WARRIOR GIRL

WARRIOR GIRL

PAULINE CHANDLER

OXFORD
UNIVERSITY PRESS

OXFORD
UNIVERSITY PRESS

Great Clarendon Street, Oxford OX2 6DP
Oxford University Press is a department of the University of Oxford.
It furthers the University's objective of excellence in research, scholarship,
and education by publishing worldwide in
Oxford New York
Auckland Cape Town Dar es Salaam Hong Kong Karachi
Kuala Lumpur Madrid Melbourne Mexico City Nairobi
New Delhi Shanghai Taipei Toronto

With offices in
Argentina Austria Brazil Chile Czech Republic France Greece
Guatemala Hungary Italy Japan South Korea Poland Portugal
Singapore Switzerland Thailand Turkey Ukraine Vietnam

Oxford is a registered trade mark of Oxford University Press
in the UK and in certain other countries

British Library Cataloguing in Publication Data
Data available

ISBN 0 19 275410 6
1 3 5 7 9 10 8 6 4 2

Typeset in MeridIen by Palimpsest Book Production Limited,
Polmont, Stirlingshire
Printed and bound in Great Britain by
Cox & Wyman Ltd, Reading, Berkshire

For Bruce

CHAPTER 1
MARIANE

It was my grandmother who saved me. I was making everyone sick with my screams, the wordless noise that said *I want my mother! I want my mother!* They were all pleading with me to stop, but I couldn't help myself. Like a hog driven to slaughter, I bit and kicked and scratched. I stuck my foot in the door of my mother's room as they tried to push me away, dug my nails into the wood of the jambs until the ends of my fingers bled, all the time making animal grunts, my eyes forever fixed on the smudge of blood, that wrongness, at the side of my mother's mouth.

Through the closing gap of the doorway I saw my aunts arranging her body, one of them wiping the blood away, as my grandmother's arms closed on mine. Her arms are as strong as steel and brook no argument. So, as she prised me away, I gave in to her, let her lead me downstairs, let her sit me on her lap as if I were a baby again. And she held me so tight that, in the end, my rage vanished and I clung to her, because I knew she was saving my life.

My mother's murderers would have cut me down too if I'd run after them. And I would have, make no mistake; I would have dashed after them straight into hell itself, to kill or to be killed, but for my grandmother.

Even though I was grown, almost ready to marry and

leave home, I submitted to the treatment: for hours she wrapped her shawl around me, and held me tight, rocking my heartache, singing. I think she expected, or, in the end, hoped, that it would bring back my voice, but it didn't.

Grandmère had a repertoire of songs which she sang to me during this time, always in the same order, one after the other, until I was soothed into sleep. My favourite was the first: *'Viens par le pré, ma belle'*, 'Come into the meadow, my pretty girl'—as I sing it again, silently in my head, I can feel grandmère's warm breath on my face and hear again the soft sound of her voice as she murmured the words. The song is imprinted on my mind like a map to tell me who I am and where I've come from. One day, I'm going home, that's my plan: when the time's right, I'll go back there, I'll just go. Of course, Uncle Jacques will try to stop me.

I was sent here because it's too dangerous for me in Reims. Well, I shan't tell him: I'll wait until he's away or busy with the harvest or until I think he's forgotten my existence, then I'll grab my bag and I'll go home. I won't let grandmère send me back again.

They say it's a long dangerous road from Domrémy to Reims, but I'll travel at night, using the ditches and tracks that no one else uses. I'll stay off the road: the English are all over it like a rash. But, anyway, even if I were seen, no one would bother with me. I'm a 'throwback', according to Uncle Jacques, a dimblebat, an idiot, because I can't speak. It makes me angry, but I don't let on. Underneath I'm stoking my rage, turning it into the energy I need to get back to Reims.

It's hot today, hot September. This field of turnips looks

small from the farmhouse, but when you're in it and not even halfway through pulling the crop, it stretches out to infinity. To be honest, I couldn't care less if I never see another turnip in my life. I've been doing this job all week, with my cousin Jehanne. Which means, more or less, by myself, because as soon as Jehanne has filled her quota of baskets, which she does at top speed, she's off into Long Meadow. She lies down in the stubble, prostrate, like a nun in a church, making the sign of the cross with her body on the ground and she lies like that, quite silent, for hours. She says she is attending to God. She says she is listening for His message. This seems devout, but it can't be right, can it?

I hate turnips. They don't even taste nice. These are purple. Last week we pulled the yellow. The leaves are so hairy and rough, turnip-pulling ruins your hands. I wish my hands were like those of Father Cornelius; his hands are as soft as lamb's wool and his eyes are deep, like brown pools on a hot summer's day. I'd like my husband to look like Father Cornelius. He's slim and strong and his face goes quite still when he looks at you, which makes you feel special. The only thing is that sometimes a cold look comes in his eyes, as if he knows all your sins and has got you signed, sealed, judged, and sent to damnation.

He'd better not find out about Jehanne lying down in the fields. He'd probably think she was showing off and getting above her station; a mere woman trying to listen to God by herself instead of in church at the proper time. He wouldn't like that, I know he wouldn't. But if he asked me about her, I couldn't lie, so he'd better not.

She's getting to her feet. I shade my eyes to get a better

view. She always knows when it's time for the bells to ring out the call to prayer and she stands facing the church, listening, as if the bells are ringing just for her.

'Mariane! Mariane!' It's Jehanne's mother, my aunt Isabeau. She's standing by the gate into the farmyard, tying a scarf round her hair. 'Where's Jehanne?'

Something's happened. She never fetches us from the fields, but she's hitched up her skirt and is treading over the ruts in the lane, crossing over to the gate. She stops and shades her eyes.

'Mariane!' I wave to show that I've heard, push floppy strands of damp hair back under my headscarf and rub the sweat from my brow, ready to pay attention. 'Where's Jehanne? I need you both back at the house.'

As if I've not heard the question, I wave again and walk down the field towards her, carrying two baskets of turnips, one in each hand.

'Where's Jehanne?' she says again.

As I get close to her, I stumble and spill my load at her feet. There are small dusty turnips rolling in every direction. Some end up in a stinking puddle, causing a cloud of shiny blue and green flies to explode into the air.

'Oh God—' she says, batting the flies away from her face, '—never mind—oh, dear—are you all right, Mariane— oh dear—never mind—' Automatically she helps me re-load the baskets, her mind obviously elsewhere.

'I'll take these,' she says finally, stowing the load under her arms. Then she says sharply, 'Fetch Jehanne. I need you both now.' As she turns away I hear her speaking to herself under her breath, as if organizing the tasks in her mind. 'We can use the dog-cart. One of them can pull it with a shoulder harness. Pray God it doesn't rain,' and then she's gone.

I climb back to where I can see Jehanne standing in the middle of the meadow, as still as a rock. Everything around her is still; the long grass, the poppies, the flax, stand as if in a painting. The insects are still and the birds. The trees look as if they're listening, or waiting, or both.

As I walk towards her I try not to make a sound, because I don't want to break the silence. Jehanne's silence. It's as if she can stop the world. I don't know how she does it, but I can feel it.

As I get close she turns slightly to look at me with that special smile of hers and the silence is broken and all the world moves again. I hear the hum of bees and the swish of the wind through the trees. As Jehanne steps forward to meet me a skylark rises from the ground at her feet. We both stop and tilt our heads, watching it soar high into the wide blue sky.

CHAPTER 2
A MAP

Aunt Isabeau's yard was crowded with men and boys, arming themselves. They were shouting and laughing, as if it were market day, not a day on which they might have to defend Domrémy against the English. Uncle Jacques was tipping a pile of clothes from the back of a cart into the middle of the yard and the lads were busy picking out the best.

They put on two or three tunics for padding, then a stiff leather jerkin on top, secured with a belt, if they could get hold of one. Then they stuck cudgels and knives in the belt, and went to sort through the boots. They pulled them on and stamped around in them, to make them fit, and never mind whether they were a pair or not.

The farmhouse was busy too. A stream of folk ducked under the stone lintel, in and out, to and fro, like frantic bees in a hive under attack. As the noise boiled up around me—chattering voices, clashing harness, clattering hooves—I turned to ask Jehanne what the news was, but we had been separated. Then I spotted her standing in the shade of a tree, on the other side of the yard, talking to one of the boys in charge of the horses. But, as I set off to join her, Aunt Isabeau signalled me into the house, so I grabbed my skirt in both hands and picked my way through the turmoil. From snatches of conversation I soon found out what all the fuss was about.

'They were a darned sight nearer this time! They fired the crop—all that good wheat gone to waste! Gone, all gone!'

'Old Thierry's vineyard was trampled, left like a midden. And they emptied the vats—yes, all of them, every last one. A river of wine ran down the street, a river, I tell you.'

'Bring me a goddam, vile English pig, here, within reach of my dagger's point—I'll whittle him into slices and carve my name on his bones!'

The story, now three days old, was that English raiders had come within fifteen miles of Domrémy. A similar band had once set the village alight, so everyone, except able-bodied men and boys, was to be evacuated immediately to the Chateau d'Île, a stronghold in the middle of the River Meuse, which runs through the town.

The boys sang war songs and chattered like birds, while their leaders discussed their plan to set an ambush on either side of the great north road, and for a few minutes I stood and watched them, frozen by memories of the night my mother was killed. That was the work of English raiders. I longed to shout out to our boys and make them listen, to warn them that these goddams were no farmers playing at war, but cruel and savage killers. But, as always, my tongue was a lump of stone and my throat closed, my voice clamped in a crushing vice.

As the horses were led into position and steadied for mounting, I ached to go with the troop. Why were girls destined to watch and wait while the men went to fight?

I could fight, I was skilled with a quarterstaff; my grand-mother had insisted that I was taught to defend myself.

And after we had defeated this band of English dogs, I could go home. My way back to Reims was along the northward road. I could go with them now, if I disguised myself. I could grab some of these clothes and put them on. They were within reach: shirts, trousers, leather jerkin. I could wear boots and stuff my hair under a cap, rub dust in my face, walk between two horses, out of sight. Then, after the fight, under cover of darkness, I could slip away and follow the road home in the moonlight.

It was at this point that my courage gave out, because of course I would be missed and pursued. And even if I could slip away in the turmoil of the evacuation, I had no idea how far it was to Reims, only that it had taken several days to get here in Uncle Jacques's cart, and I would be on foot. What about food? Maybe I should be like Jehanne and trust to God to look after me.

But grandmère would say that was foolish: God helps those who help themselves.

I thought again about her and my home. Was she safe? What would I find when I got back? My peaceful home or a smoking ruin? It was the not knowing that hurt me: it pricked me like a thorn at every turn.

As I watched the men mount up, I slowly clenched my fists, saying over and over to myself that my day would come.

'Jeannot!' Jehanne was suddenly at my elbow, calling to one of the boys, who was washing himself in the horse trough. Jean Lebecq, a neighbour's son. Why was he here? He was scarcely out of his baby skirts.

Jeannot lifted his head, dripping, and grinned from ear to ear when he saw Jehanne, then pushed folk aside to get to her. As he gave her a great hug, I laughed at the sight: he, thin and weedy, she, big-boned and strong as an ox. She almost buried him.

'Jeannot! Jeannot! What on earth are you doing here?' she said.

'I'm going off with the soldiers. Don't look at me like that: Père said I could. And don't call me Jeannot. I'm a man now.'

'But, Jeannot, little one, my baby cousin—' She ducked as Jeannot swung his fist at her head, then laughed a great belly laugh, saying, 'But, Jeannot, I'm so much taller than you!' And she seized the dagger from his belt, stood against the door jamb and measured her height, nicking the timber in the place where the top of her head rested. 'See?'

Good-naturedly Jeannot allowed himself to be measured in the same way. 'See? You're this much shorter,' she said, measuring the span of her hand. Jeannot wouldn't look, only snatched her wrist and took back his dagger, but when she ruffled his hair, he couldn't stop himself smiling. 'Shouldn't I go to fight the English and let you stay here?' said Jehanne.

In answer, Jeannot drew himself up to his full height and his proud stance brought tears to my eyes.

'You're big, Jehanne, but you're a girl,' he said. 'Girls don't fight. It's the men's job to fight. You just leave it to us.' Jehanne laughed and hugged him again, then let him go.

As she turned into the house, I saw the smile fade from her face. I could guess her thoughts: she's as strong as any man. I've seen her tackle a cow with one of its horns stuck in the side of the stall. Had Jean Lebecq been a little older, she might have challenged him to a bout of armwrestling and made him swallow his words.

If these were her thoughts, she didn't show any resentment, but waited calmly inside the house for her mother's instructions.

Jehanne is always so patient. If she knew how I ache for revenge, I know what she would say: that vengeance is for God to deliver, and we must wait. Oh, but it's hard.

As I joined Jehanne at the table, Aunt Isabeau came from the byre into the kitchen, clutching a pile of grain sacks.

'Jehanne, we must fill these. Quickly now. There's bread and cheese. Use up the apples too. There's some on the rafters, take those first, then get the rest from the barrel. Mariane, fill some flagons with wine. Use the cask under the window in the buttery. Hurry.'

We had barely started our tasks before the bright rectangle of the doorway was darkened by the squat figure of my uncle Jacques. He went to stand behind Jehanne who was reaching down a tray of apples from the rafters. Slowly she put back the tray and turned to face him.

'What do you call this, girl?' he said, showing her the padded shirt that he wears under his breastplate. Furious, he thrust it under her nose.

'*Tu paresseuse!* Lazy baggage! You should attend to your duties here, instead of always on your knees at the church. God can wait—I can't!'

'Jacques!' Aunt Isabeau gasped and clutched the silver crucifix that hung at her neck, but Jehanne simply bowed her head, then raised it to look him straight in the eye as he fisted open a long gash in the padded fabric. A thick tuft of tow poked out of it.

Jehanne sat at the table and opened the lid of her thread box. 'I'll mend it now, père,' she said. 'It can be done in five minutes.'

With an explosive sound of disgust he pushed the shirt against her chest. 'The English could be here in five minutes,' he said, then stalked out of the house.

Dieu au ciel! I would have scrunched the shirt up into a ball and thrown it to the floor, or at least kicked my chair over, but Jehanne, patient as ever, threaded a needle and began the repair.

Uncle Jacques is always finding an excuse to quarrel with her. There's been trouble between them ever since Jehanne refused to marry the man he picked out for her. I wonder if she made the right decision? She would have had her own farm by now and left her bullying father behind. So why did she refuse? Perhaps the man was old and ugly, in which case I shouldn't blame her.

I was in the buttery filling the last of the flagons when I heard Jehanne's brother Pierre come into the house. He was in charge of the evacuation. Had he come for us? Was everyone else ready? I put a stopper in the last flagon, then picked them all up in a basket and walked to the kitchen door. I was about to go through when I heard Pierre say, 'Uncle Durand is ready: you only have to say the word!' I put down my wine and listened, but no one spoke, so I peeped through a crack in the door.

Finishing the repair to her father's shirt, Jehanne bit off the thread and stood up, presumably to take the shirt outside to her father. But Aunt Isabeau appeared and said, 'I'll take that, Jehanne. You get on with the rations.'

As Aunt Isabeau left, I saw Jehanne and Pierre exchange a very strange look, as if they were conspirators. I pressed my eye to the crack and watched as Pierre stealthily unrolled a map made of fine leather and spread it out on the table.

'Where are they now?' whispered Jehanne, poring over it, standing next to him so that the map was hidden from anyone coming in through the front door.

'There are English troops here and here,' said Pierre, tapping his finger on the map.

'Main forces or scouting parties?'

'Reconnaissance, we think, but Reims could be the next target.' Pierre laid his hands flat on either side of the map. 'You won't leave until we get back from Chateau d'Île, will you? I'll join you as soon as possible but I've promised père that I'll see everyone safely there and back.'

'I've had no message about leaving, but it must be soon. Some things are clear. I must go to Chinon, but first I must go to Vaucouleurs, to see the Sire de Baudricourt. I just don't know when.'

Chinon? That was where the Dauphin had his court. The Sire de Baudricourt was the Dauphin's man.

'Do you have to wait to be told?'

'Yes,' Jehanne sighed.

Told what? By whom?

'I'll let Uncle Durand know as soon as I know.'

'I pray it's soon.'

'How far is Burey from Vaucouleurs?'

Burey? Durand Lassois, the man they called 'Uncle', lived there. He was husband to Aunt Isabeau's niece.

Jehanne tried to find the village on the map, tracing lines with her forefinger, but, unable to read the names, faltered, thumping the map with her fist. 'I hate having to tell all these lies!'

'Steady,' said Pierre, calmly pointing to the village. 'There, look. It's only a mile or two.'

Jehanne's shoulders dropped as she sighed again, and Pierre put his arm round her and laid his head on top of hers.

'Don't worry. Père will give you his blessing when he understands.' He looked at the map again. 'From Burey we'll go as soon as possible to see de Baudricourt.'

'Yes.'

Pierre put both arms round Jehanne and held her tight. 'Aren't you even a little bit excited?'

With a serious face, Jehanne pulled away. 'This isn't a game, Pierre. It's God's plan, not mine.'

'Of course.'

Jehanne pointed to the map.

'Chinon. Orleans. Reims.'

'Reims,' repeated Pierre.

Jehanne was going to Reims? I paused, then then hurled myself through the door.

The two figures looked up startled as I made my entrance. I thrust my slate at Jehanne, with its frantically scribbled message.

Reims—take me with you.

CHAPTER THREE
MISSION

Startled, Pierre rolled up the map. Jehanne glanced at my slate with its message, then silently passed it to him. She can't read words. Her eyes were fixed on me, so I darted forward and snatched the map from the table, then unrolled it and stabbed at the mark for Reims. Then I pointed at my chest, then tugged her sleeve and pulled her to the door, so that finally she understood.

Pierre's head dropped in a hopeless gesture as he passed the slate back to her. With slow deliberate strokes, she rubbed out my message with her forefinger.

'What does she know?' Pierre said in an urgent whisper, speaking to her over my head. Vigorously I stepped between them. I shrugged my shoulders and spread my hands wide.

'Nothing. She knows nothing,' said Jehanne. She put her hand on my shoulder. 'But she wants to go back home, to Reims. It's becoming dangerous for Grandmère Alys to be alone.'

'Better to fetch grandmère here then. What use for little Mariane to go back?' I gave a furious roar and jutted my chin.

'Not so little, Pierre. Mariane is a fighter. She can hold her own against any of us.' Grinning Pierre threw a mock-punch at my shoulder and I easily knocked the blow aside. 'When père brought Mariane here,' Jehanne went on,

'Grandmère Alys refused to move, saying she would never let the English drive her from her home. She has two daughters living close by and, to all accounts, she's done very well so far, tipping dead rats into the well that the English use, then selling remedies for "French belly". The English call her mother.'

Pierre laughed out loud at this and so did I.

Jehanne paused to wipe the slate quite clean on a corner of her apron, then handed it back to me.

'You can read words as well as write them?' she said.

I nodded.

To Pierre, she said, 'We might have need of a scribe.'

As they turned to leave, I touched Jehanne's arm, hoping for a decision, but gently she disengaged my hand and said, 'Later.' So I huffed and stamped my foot, and shoved my slate back into the pocket inside my shift.

Laughing, Jehanne said, 'Be patient, Mariane. And save your spirit. If you come with me, you'll need it.' Then she bent to kiss my cheek, before turning away to get on with evacuating the farm.

From the doorway I watched them, going over Jehanne's words. Something had snagged my thoughts, something I'd heard but not understood, something important. *Save your spirit . . . you'll need it.* Was the journey to Reims so dangerous? The present threat to Domrémy was from a few ruffians. Uncle Jacques would soon deal with them: everyone knew the evacuation was only a practice for any future attack.

We have been at war with the English all of my life. My own father, a loyal knight of the last French king, poor mad King Charles, died at the treacherous hands of the English, injured at the battle of Agincourt.

I never knew him: I was born on the day that he died, All Saints Day, November 1st, in the year of Our Lord 1415: but the name Agincourt always burns in my thoughts. Over six thousand Frenchmen were massacred that day, drawn into an English trap. And, stained with their blood, the English king, Henry V, took the throne.

But now the English king is dead, and the throne of France is held by Bully Bedford as regent for Henry's son, little Henry VI. The English prowl the whole of the north like wolves. It shames me to say that they have French allies, the followers of the Duke of Burgundy, who hopes to share power in a France ruled by an English king. 'Better a strong country under an English king, than a weak one under the dauphin,' they say. 'We are all cousins, we all share the blood of William the Conqueror. Why not join England and France?'

I shudder to think of it, but it could happen. If the so-called Anglo-Burgundians take Angers or Orléans, the south will fall and France, my beloved country, will be no more.

The dauphin Charles, who should be the king, hides away with his friends. It is hard for him to stake a claim: after his father's death, his German mother allied with the English and barred him from the succession. But he is French and of royal blood, he is the true heir. If only he would show himself and act like a king, he would gather support, I know he would.

I will never accept an English king. There is no honour in the English. The shadowy face of my mother's assailant loomed in front of my mind and my thoughts were blades: *English dog. God help you if I ever see you again.* My pulse raced, my right arm jerked as I held up an imaginary dagger and plunged it home.

Steadily I lowered my arm and took deep breaths and reminded myself that my first goal was to get back to Reims, to look after my grandmother.

There was something I had missed in the conversation between Pierre and Jehanne. I tried to recall the details of all I had heard.

What does she know? Nothing. She knows nothing.

What was there to know? Something the two of them wanted kept secret, some plan that, judging by the flash of panic on Pierre's face, they were desperate to keep to themselves.

They had pored over that map like two military commanders. Was it something to do with the war then? Surely they weren't planning to fight the English? Pierre maybe: it was the sort of reckless stunt lots of young men had tried. But Jehanne? *She doesn't know, does she?* Pierre had spoken to her as if she were in charge of the secret. Jehanne wasn't planning a military campaign, was she? Captain Jehanne, riding off to save France on the back of an old brown cow. I laughed out loud at the absurdity of my thoughts.

'Is the wine ready yet?' Aunt Isabeau appeared in the doorway and my thoughts scattered like water on a griddle.

'Almost,' I said and hurried back to my task.

It took all day to get everyone to safety within the walls of the stronghold at Chateau d'Île. The sun set at our backs as we waited in line to board the ferry. A whole village:

men, women, and children; the sick and the healthy. Most were carrying bundles and baggage, trundling carts, driving animals, down to the crossing point, then camping on the river bank to wait their turn. A whole village on alert, now reduced in the twilight to a seething mass of shapes, silent except for the racking coughs of the sick, and the babies' hungry cries.

Jehanne and her brothers had ridden the cows like horses, as outriders to the column, and I'd soon lost sight of them. Aunt Isabeau had left me, to attend a girl near her time, so I had walked most of the journey alone.

I found a dryish spot and sat down, slipping my bundle from my back. It contained all my worldly possessions: some clothes wrapped round the book grandmère used to teach me to read, a spoon and a knife. Not a very sharp knife but useful for cutting bread or cheese. Under one arm, I carried my pet hen, Polly, safely tucked up in a piece of hessian sacking. Only her head poked out and with every jolt and stumble of the journey her bright eyes sparked a reproach. Now I took her on to my lap and calmed her by stroking her neck feathers. She struggled a little to get free, but I held her tight and whispered, 'Not far now, Poll. We'll soon be there.' Empty words of comfort, because I had never been to the island bolt-hole before and I had no idea what to expect, but I repeated my grand-mother's sayings: *'Travel hopefully: fear of what is to come is your worst enemy.'*

Thinking of grandmère made me sad, so I focused instead on the bobbing light of the ferry lantern as it made its way back to us across the Meuse. It was an eerie sight and reminded me of the story about the river Styx, that black river of forgetting that stretches between our world and the Land of the Dead. I shuddered and hugged Polly close, then said my prayers. And I was glad when the ferry crunched on to the gravel of the stony shore and old Nicolas, the boatman, jumped out cursing because his backside was wet.

The Chateau d'Île was a filthy place. We were safe enough within its walls, but it was open to all weathers, and we were crammed together with the animals—the stench was rank. Jehanne and I found a place next to a wall and made ourselves comfortable, spreading straw for our beds, side by side, on the ground. I stowed Polly on a pile of sweet smelling hay, in a wooden crate under the ledge, and gave her water and grain and a cabbage leaf to peck at. She was still cross from the journey and made disapproving clucks, especially when there was no perch for her to rest on. I promised to improve her quarters as soon as I could.

That night, listening to the snores and snorts of the company and the constant shifting and shuffling of the cows tied to their pegs, I tried to settle myself to sleep, as I always did, by silently sharing the day with grandmère. I had fixed my eyes overhead, right up at the stars, and I was telling her about Pierre's map, describing it in great detail: 'Light brown goat-hide I think, beaten to fine leather. Pierre had drawn the lines of the the roads and rivers in different inks. There was a big red spot to mark the city . . .' Then I heard Jehanne. She had slipped off her bed and was kneeling by it, resting her head on her joined hands, as if she were praying. I twisted my head, trying to catch what she was saying, because it didn't sound like any prayer I knew.

'Ave Maria. Maria. Maria. Forgive me. Forgive me. Holy Saint Catherine. Forgive me.' Jehanne pressed her forehead hard with her fingertips. There was a long pause, then she put her hands together and started to pray again, speaking the words in a measured way, as if she had gathered herself under better control.

'Holy Saint Catherine. Please forgive me. I'm such a coward, I know, but I'm at a loss. This is too great a task for somebody like me. How can I command men-at-arms? I want to do as you ask, but truly, the thought of it makes me weak. A warhorse? Armour? How can I?' Jehanne sighed as if her heart were breaking, then covered her face with her hands, pressing until her knuckles showed white.

I was on the point of reaching out to her when she took her hands away and looked up. I looked past her into the shadows, to see what she could see, but try as I might I couldn't see anything. She seemed to be listening. After a long minute, as if repeating instructions, she murmured, '"Vaucouleurs". "Messire de Baudricourt".' Then she bowed her head and, with hands clasped again, whispered, 'Take the first step and the rest will follow. The Lord shall preserve thy going out and thy coming in—'

In my mind, I joined in with the rest: From this time forth, and for evermore. Amen. This prayer I knew.

After that Jehanne's shoulders sagged and her head drooped to her chest as if she had come through a great struggle, then, with another weary sigh, she turned to sit on the edge of her straw bed.

Minutes later, she raised her head and looked at me,

and patted the straw at her side. Shocked, I went to sit with her, embarrassed that I'd been caught watching.

But Jehanne was kind and took both my hands in hers. Then she began to speak.

'I want you to listen carefully, Mariane. What I have to say will seem strange and perhaps impossible to believe, but I want you to know that it's true. You have already guessed that I'm leaving Domrémy. I shall tell you why, because—' She paused and gently touched my forehead with her fingers, '—because I believe you are meant to be told.

'This must be kept secret. Few others know, maman and Pierre do, no one else, not here anyway. Above all, my father must not find out, because he would certainly stop me from leaving. So, Mariane, you must swear to say nothing.'

In a childish way I nodded eagerly, anxious to hear the secret, but when Jehanne dropped my hands to pass me her rosary, I saw that she was deadly serious. This was no child's play. Jehanne's face was set like adamant as she repeated her request: 'Swear.'

So I took the cross, kissed it reverently and passed it back. Without words, the gesture would have to do. Jehanne put the rosary aside, took my hands again and pressed them hard.

'Listen, then, and don't interrupt—you will want to, believe me—because what I have to say is hard to accept, for me too. All I ask is that you listen.'

I nodded and waited for her to get on with the secret. What was so terrible? Why was she so reluctant to speak?

Still holding my hands, I should say almost clinging to

them, Jehanne looked round at the sleeping forms that filled the enclosure, then, satisfied that no one was awake to hear, she said, 'I am going away. I have to leave. Soon.' She bent her head low over mine. 'I'm not sure of the day or the hour. I don't know that yet, but I . . . I will be told.'

'*I will be told* . . .' Who by?

I gasped and started, jumping to the conclusion that she must be a spy, involved in a deep conspiracy.

'Not a sound,' she said, then, pursing her lips, 'it's so difficult to tell you. Are you ready to hear? Is it fair to give you this burden? Yet it seems right, because you may have a part to play.' She seemed to be talking to herself and I was getting frightened, but I held up my head, determined not to show it.

'Mariane, do you believe in God? Are you a true Christian? Do you love our Lord, the Saviour, with all your heart and mind? To your last breath?'

I shrank back, puzzled. In my experience it's only charlatans who need to profess their faith so loudly. And, to be honest, I wasn't sure I could answer yes to these serious questions. But since 'yes' was required for Jehanne to go on with the secret, I nodded as fervently as I could.

Then it came, the thunderbolt.

'Mariane, I have been given a mission.' I stared at her face, lit by moonlight, white, luminous, unearthly pale, and pressed my dry lips together. *Mission*. The word rang in my ears like a bell. It was the word that I hadn't been able to remember, the word that had snagged me when I had listened to Jehanne talking to Pierre, as they studied the map. It was such a powerful word. I held my breath as Jehanne went on, 'God has given me a task.'

Was that all? I breathed again. I thought she was going to say the dauphin had given her special orders. God I could cope with.

'I know it's hard to accept, that He should choose me, single me out to do such—oh,' she sighed, 'such deeds.' She looked away and stared down at her hands clasped tightly in her lap. When I could stand the waiting no longer, I touched her hands to prompt her to go on. *What deeds?*

As if she had returned from a long journey or had woken up from a deep sleep, Jehanne slowly rubbed her face with her hands and turned to face me.

'Mariane,' she said solemnly, 'God has called me to perform a great task, sending his message through our own Saint Catherine, Saint Margaret, and Saint Michael.'

I frowned. *How?*

'All of them speak to me,' she said. At this I bridled and pulled back. 'No, wait. Listen, listen.' She caught my hands again and held them. 'Please hear me out. This isn't a recent event. I've heard the voices over many years.'

At this I laughed out loud—my grating laugh noise—broke free and touched her forehead, pretending to wipe the fever away. I knew someone else who heard voices: a beggar who squatted in a filthy back street behind the cathedral in Reims. We knew he was ill: grandmère and I used to take medicine to him.

'Thank you but I'm quite well. And quite serious.' And, lowering her voice, she repeated her claim, in firm slow words like the strokes of a hammer.

'God has spoken to me, through his messengers. Mariane, you know how I leave you sometimes when we're out in the fields? You've seen me, haven't you? When I'm out there alone? But I'm not alone. They come to me. Blessed Saint Catherine—yes, our own Saint Catherine—and Saint Margaret. But the greatest wonder of all, Saint Michael comes to me. God's own warrior, his archangel. How can I refuse to do as he asks? He has spoken to me, Mariane. He has given me my mission.'

I stared and shrugged. I spread my hands to ask the question, 'What mission?'

She went on, 'I have to go to the dauphin, Charles, at Chinon, and make sure he is publicly crowned King of France in the cathedral at Reims, so that the pride of France is restored and heart put back into her people. I have to raise the siege of Orléans and drive the English back, back across the sea.'

Her face was alight, her eyes gleaming, her lips working on the words, shivering with excitement as she pronounced them, but I was paralyzed, unable to take it all in. It was a fantasy, a fairy tale. Crown a king? Raise a siege? What madness was this? Poor Jehanne. She really believed it, she really did.

I dropped her hands like hot coals and backed away, shaking my head, and, God forgive me, crossing myself.

'Mariane.' She tried to take my hands again.

Nnaaaaaaggghhhh. The growl came out more fiercely than I'd intended and Jehanne, startled, gripped my wrist, at the same time scanning the sleepers to see if anyone had been disturbed by the noise.

'If you can't believe me,' she said, put it out of your mind. Try to forget what I've said. Call it brain sickness if you will. I didn't believe it myself at first. The voices came to me years ago, but I didn't tell anyone. It's taken this long for my faith to grow and become strong enough to carry me through what I have to do. Imagine, God choosing me, a farm girl who can't read, who's never been further than the next village, who's never even carried a sword. What do I know about warfare or crowning a king? It's beyond me.' She sat back.

'But what I do know is how I feel inside.' She knocked her fist against her chest. 'How can I stand against Him? God's power is limitless. All I had to do in the end was submit to that.'

She watched me, with shining eyes. *Jehanne* . . . how I longed to speak to her, to reason with her, to rout her fantasy with rational argument.

I shook my head and she put her hand over mine. It was a plea for understanding, a plea for help. *'Be with me.'*

'Mariane. You may have a part to play,' she murmured.

God help us, I prayed. I closed my eyes. This was madness. I have never made a rash decision in my life. Grandmère drummed it into me: *'Weigh the odds! Work out the consequences! Above all, sleep on it! A clear mind comes with fresh air in the morning!'*

I could not follow Jehanne on this mad venture. My place was with grandmère. I moved uneasily.

'The journey will be long and difficult,' Jehanne said. 'I'll be glad of your company. A strong arm and a friendly face.'

I looked out at the dark mass of the stronghold with its sleeping inhabitants, my thoughts twisting like eels.

Jehanne saw my confusion.

'Go to Reims. Attend your grandmother. We shall travel

together as far as Vaucouleurs—will you help me seek an audience with the sire?'

I nodded.

'Afterwards—' She shrugged—'God willing, I shall journey to Chinon.' She put her hand over mine. 'Be in Reims when I arrive to crown the king. I ask no more.'

I gasped and covered my face with my hands. Had she seen the doubt in my eyes?' Shamed, I rocked forward and the neck of my shirt fell open.

'What's that?' Jehanne lifted the key and chain that I wore and twisted it in the moonlight.

I snatched the key from her fingers.

'Something from home?'

I jutted my chin, refusing to meet her eyes.

'That important, huh?' she said.

I stayed frozen, keeping a tight hold on the key.

'You must go home, Mariane. That first.'

She paused, staring into the darkness.

'You don't want to stay here, do you, far from the life you were born to lead?'

I turned to her and shook my head.

'Neither do I.'

CHAPTER FOUR
THE JOURNEY BEGINS

It was December before Jehanne could leave Domrémy. In the autumn months following our return from Chateau d'Île, she and Pierre laid their plans. The first step was to seek the support of the Sire de Baudricourt, the military governor of Vaucouleurs. It was Aunt Isabeau who had thought of visiting her niece in the village of Burey, not two miles from there.

On her return she brought news that her niece's husband, 'Uncle' Durand would speak to the Sire on her behalf.

Knowing that Jehanne's father would never allow her to go off on such a wild venture, Uncle Durand agreed to a deception: he would invite Jehanne to Burey, to stay with him and his wife during the winter, to help with the new baby. As soon as possible in the new year, Pierre would collect Jehanne and bring her home. She would be back in Domrémy for Lent.

It was a lie. If Jehanne convinced the Sire de Baudricourt to support her mission, she would have set out for Chinon by then. As for me, with the English threatening Domrémy now, it was easy to gain permission to return home to Reims.

But Jehanne hated lying to her father and when the time came to leave she could hardly bear to speak to him.

* * *

We left at night to avoid being seen by the English. Samson, Uncle Durand's big black dray-horse, snorted and whinnied as his master tightened his hold on the reins. His hooves clopped and dinged on the cobbles of the farmyard, striking sparks as Uncle Durand walked him back to Jehanne, who sat hunched in her cloak, head covered and bowed, astride Caesar, her stout brown cob.

I mounted Caesar behind her, adjusting my shoulder-strap to position Polly in her basket securely at my side. Uncle Durand went to open the gate for us. 'Don't worry,' he said in a loud voice, 'Vaucouleurs isn't far . . .'

'Sh!' Pierre warned, as an arrow of light lanced the dark. The farmhouse door sprang open and there, silhouetted against the light, stood Uncle Jacques.

'Jehanne! You'll be home for Lent,' he called.

'Yes, père,' came the muffled voice.

'Bring me some of Durand's fine blackberry wine!'

'Yes.'

'Speak up, child! What ails thee?' Uncle Jacques took a step towards her and put his stockinged foot in a puddle.

'God's bones!' He hopped back to the threshold, then called again. 'Bring some of his best cheese, if you can wheedle it out of him!'

'Yes, père.'

'Well, go then. No, wait!' He dug deep in a pocket and started forward, ignoring the puddles. 'Here! Take some ginger with you.' He reached up and pressed a small bag into her hand. 'Just a little, to warm you in cold weather.'

'Thank you, père.'

'À Dieu, then.' He reached up and kissed her awkwardly on both cheeks, then stepped back. 'Take no unnecessary risks. Turn back at the first sign of trouble! Go then. *À Dieu. À Dieu!*'

Then, suddenly, 'Wait, Durand! Wait!' he called angrily. 'I'm not happy about this. I'm coming with you.'

Aunt Isabeau joined him. 'They can't wait for you, Jacques. And you've no boots on! What are you thinking of? They don't need you—Pierre's with them, and Durand! Off you go!' Waving to us over her shoulder, she drew Uncle Jacques towards the house. 'I need you here,' she said. 'There are rats in the henhouse again, I've heard them.'

On the threshold, Uncle Jacques stopped to glance back. He shrugged and said, 'You see how it is, Durand. Pierre, you have a blade?' Behind me, Pierre's horse clip-clopped from the shadows. Pierre tapped his sword. '*À Dieu* then.' I breathed a shuddery breath. *Please, God, make him go.* 'Jehanne, be sure to send word from Burey.'

Jehanne twisted round in the saddle, but Uncle Durand answered for her as he pulled hard on her reins. 'We will.' Then Caesar was moving through the gate and the farm-house door finally closed. *Merci, bon Dieu.* I breathed again. And that's how our journey began.

It was the time of year between Christmas and Epiphany, when the world seems asleep. The time between Jesus's birth and the Wise Men's coming, when everyone waits to learn if the stable child is really the Saviour of the world. The time, too, when, no matter what trouble you face, you can make a fresh start.

I have always thrilled to a journey and I patted Polly's

basket with a light heart as we rode out into the night. I was looking forward to going home. To see grandmère again! Heartsease.

But my thoughts came back, time and again, to Jehanne's words: 'You may have a part to play.' If her mission were God's design, was there really some task for me? I wished I knew it. Grandmère's voice cut through my thoughts like true steel. *'The future's a desert land, Mariane, with no signposts, no certainties. Keep your thoughts to the present.'*

Bien sûr, mamie. So, I would accompany Jehanne to Burey, then go on to Reims. And leave the rest up to God.

It was a bitter cold night. Frost rimed the thatch of the pig pens at Lane End, and as we passed, moonlight gleamed on the icicles hanging from their eaves. It was hard going. The horses' hooves slipped on the ice or tipped in the ruts, tossing us about like little boats in a storm.

Perched on Caesar's back, behind Jehanne, with Polly's basket banging gently against my thigh, I struggled to stay upright, so as not to add weight to Jehanne's shoulders. She seemed exhausted already, quite limp and listless, and rode with her head down, as we made snail's progress along the long white road that led us to Vaucouleurs.

The lies she had told weighed heavily. I don't suppose she knew when, or if, she would see Domrémy again. Her father had no idea of her mission. He knew nothing about Vaucouleurs or Chinon. Let alone Orléans, where she planned to raise the siege. Or Reims, where she would crown the king. No, the deception worked like fat on a hinge. But Jehanne was heartsick, and in my head I muttered angry words to God about it all.

'She knows this is Your idea, but, lying to her father? It's not a very good start, is it? Look at her: this is breaking her heart, and she's only just begun. Well? What are You going to do about it? At least show her a sign or something. Amen.'

As you may know, God doesn't always answer straight away, which isn't surprising when you consider how busy He is, and nothing much altered for the first few miles of our ride.

I tried to see a sign in the stars, blue-white in the black sky, but they blurred as I looked up, my eyes seared to tears by the cold, and I shivered and wiggled my fingers through the bars of Polly's wicker basket to stroke her feathers, grateful for her warmth.

I jerked awake when the horse slowed then staggered as it trod carefully down a narrow gully and into a wide flat glade bounded by trees.

'Well done, Caesar, lad, well done, my fine boy.' Jehanne's low whisper calmed the horse as she slipped from the saddle and threw the reins over his head, releasing the bit.

I dismounted, gingerly feeling the backs of my thighs and wishing I had a bit of goose fat to ease the saddle sores. Then I unstrapped Polly and made sure she had food and water.

Uncle Durand, who had been reconnoitering the surrounding wood, came striding back.

'Time to eat and sleep, Mariane. Here—' I caught the rough blanket. 'Wrap up tight in that: we daren't risk a fire.'

Within minutes the four of us were sitting huddled round a plain horn lantern that shone a dim but comforting light.

'We must keep warm,' said Pierre, passing me a wineskin.

I smiled my thanks and took a deep draught of the wine, then wished I hadn't because it tasted like neat boar's blood, thick and sour. But an inner heat soon spread to my fingers and toes. And when Jehanne broke the bread and passed it to us, I grinned and hiccupped. 'Save some for me,' said Uncle Durand, reaching over to take back the wine. Jehanne, as usual, didn't take any wine, but drank water, then she pulled her blanket tight around her and settled herself to sleep.

The others were soon asleep, but as time passed, I grew more wide awake and alert to every sound. The lantern burnt low, then the flame snapped out, and the darkness swallowed us up like a huge black wave.

It was then that I heard the crack of a twig; near, too near for comfort. My head grew large with listening, ears pricked, tight as a singing cord. *Crack* . . . then again, softer but unmistakable, the sound of creeping footsteps. As I reached into the dark to warn Uncle Durand, they were upon us.

Somebody grabbed my arms and dragged them behind my back, to tie them, but I roared loudly from the bottom of my lungs, startling him with my shouts, then kicked his shin, and my attacker cursed and loosened his grip. 'God's teeth! It's a hell cat!'

English! Fury made me strong and I pulled myself free. I fell over the lantern but, recovering in a single move, picked it up and swung it wide in front of me. *Thwack*! It caught the side of my assailant's head and, groaning, he fell.

'Run! Run!' shouted Pierre, brandishing his sword to keep the attackers at bay, and shoving me roughly behind him. Jehanne was with me as I turned and ran into the wood. Then, as we struggled to release the horses, there were lights, lanterns, coming towards us through the trees like will-o'-the-wisps, and shouts from a band of new arrivals to their friends, our attackers. And in the half-light I saw Jehanne stand to meet them, with her feet planted like a wrestler, strong and sure.

I ran to help, but, as one of them lunged at her, she twisted her shoulder into him and, using his own speed against him, flung him away. To my amazement, there he was on the ground, making no sign of getting up again.

Uncle Durand took charge then and shoved us deep into a thicket where we could stay hidden as the English kicked through the remains of our camp.

I parted the branches to watch as another man appeared. A black shadow on horseback. He seemed to be the leader, arriving to hear their report, so that I realized that this attack was no casual event. English soldiers had been sent after us. Why? Did someone know of Jehanne's mission? Were they trying to stop her?

The soldiers gathered to meet him. One raised a lantern and by its light I saw the leader flourish a dagger and press it to the throat of one of his own men. The blade glinted. Rubies were set in a line from hilt to point, like drops of blood. The weapon blazed wealth and power. This man was no backstreet ruffian. He put the dagger away and gave a furious roar as the soldiers fluffed their excuses, then he spurred the sides of his horse, pulling angrily at the bit, so that it reared as he forced it back the way he had come. It was cruel treatment and my blood boiled. I made to leap after him but Uncle Durand held me back.

'Let them go,' he muttered as the men trudged back through the forest. 'Save your strength.'

I dropped to my knees and stared after the English dogs, until no sight or sound of them remained. But as we made a fresh camp, I found a stout stick for myself and shoved it into my belt, across my back. If we were attacked again, I would make them pay.

We set off at dawn. No one else seemed concerned about the attack: their talk was of Vaucouleurs; but, in the grey morning light, my thoughts flew inevitably to when I had met English thugs before, on the day of my mother's death.

Maman, grandmère, and I had been in the kitchen as usual. The sun shone in stripes on the table top where grandmère and maman were potting honey. The enjoyment was spoiled only by some hornets who seemed to be attracted to the sweetness. I was supposed to be helping but I was enjoying the warmth of the sun on the backs of my hands and putting first one then the other in and out of the sunbeams.

'Ah!' said maman, flailing her arm. 'These hornets! Agh!'

'You've been stung? Garlic, Mariane. Crushed in milk,' grandmère said. 'It will dull the pain.'

As I pounded the garlic, I heard the soldiers in the yard.

They didn't bother disguising their approach; they couldn't have anyway, drink made them clumsy. One of them rapped on the door then flung it open.

Maman shrieked, but grandmère, calm always, simply twisted slightly on her stool, so that she was facing the door as they piled inside. There were six of them. We had no chance.

Fear made me icy calm. I didn't look at them, but went on with my task.

'What's here?' said one in broken French, taking my dish.

'Crushed garlic in milk. My mother's been stung by a hornet. This eases the pain.'

'Does it now?'

It happened in an instant, and yet slowly as if in a dream. Maman's chair fell backwards as she was pulled out of it. The lamp swung to and fro, as her arm knocked it in passing. Two of the soldiers pushed maman back to the wall, while the others ransacked the house.

'Where is it? Tell us. Where is it?'

They bore down on maman like hounds but she wouldn't speak. Her body bent away from them, her fists clamped to her chest, tight under her throat, her lips sealed. Her eyes blazed her defiance.

'Villains!' I roared, but grandmère grabbed me, pressed her hand over my mouth, and bundled me to the back door.

She pressed a key into my hand. 'Run!' she hissed. 'Run!'

The door was behind me, partly open. I had only to squeeze through the gap. But I dug in my heels, unwilling to leave, and watched over grandmère's restraining arm the soldiers manhandling my mother.

They, who stank worse than beasts, pulled back her bright hair that smelt of violets; their faces, greasy with sweat, their foul breath tainted her rose-coloured cheeks.

Grandmère's fingers pushed me like steel. 'There's nothing you can do!' she whispered urgently. 'Go! Take the key—go!'

So, my heart breaking, I took off, holding the key tight in my fist as I ran. The path into the wood was clear. It led eventually to the highway. Escape lay before me and I ran partway down the path then stopped, knowing that I couldn't run and leave them. Not if it cost me my life.

By this time, folk in the houses nearby were coming out to see what the disturbance was.

'Who's there? Who is it? What's happening?'

Aunt Renée caught me by the arm as I ran past, back into the yard.

'Mariane! What is it?'

'Soldiers,' I said. 'English.'

'*Dieu*. Soldiers. English.' The whispers ran through the gathering crowd like wildfire. I looked round, from face to face. All women. The men were away, up the hill, planting the long acres that week.

Suddenly our cottage door was flung open and the soldiers left, one stopping to urinate on the haystack at the end of the garden.

When he had gone, I walked towards the open door of the cottage. There was no sound from inside. As I walked slowly forwards, I felt my two aunts, Thérèse and Renée, my mother's sisters, step out of the crowd to stand on either side of me, and we went into the cottage together.

Grandmère stood at the the foot of the steps, making

repetitive signs with her hand, like a broken clockwork. My aunts pushed past me to get to her, then went on up the steps into the back room. That's when I howled out loud: 'Maman!' and rushed after them.

Maman was lying on the bed, blood at the side of her mouth and slowly staining the front of her dress over her heart. Her eyes were closed. She seemed asleep, but I knew that she was dead. Thérèse took her hand and said, 'She should have told them.'

Renée replied, 'It wouldn't have stopped them.'

I looked up as grandmère joined me in the doorway.

'Mother,' said Thérèse, looking past me at grandmère. 'Where's the key?'

Grandmère, still not speaking, took hold of my closed fist and opened it.

All four of us looked at the key and I opened my mouth to ask why my mother had been murdered. I tried, several times, to ask this question, but it was as if the hand of God had reached down and taken my voice away.

'Mariane?' The soft sound of Jehanne calling my name settled over my painful thoughts like cool balm. I looked up, surprised out of my memories. She gestured to the stray houses lit by the rising sun. Uncle Durand and Pierre were ahead of us.

'Burey,' she said. 'We're nearly there.'

CHAPTER FIVE
VAUCOULEURS

I was furious. Robert, Sire de Baudricourt, military commander of the whole region? The governor of Vaucouleurs, the dauphin's representative, with hundreds of soldiers at his beck and call? After waiting at his gate for a week, I thought he was nothing but a fat pig, with hairy ears and a pimply snout. And that was insulting to pigs.

On the day we arrived, Uncle Durand went to the castle to present Jehanne's petition. The Sire de Baudricourt would scarcely listen. He laughed heartily, and advised Uncle Durand to send his niece home with a beating. The next day Uncle Durand tried again, but the sire would not see Jehanne. When he was asked a third time to grant her an audience, Milord High-and-Mighty threatened to beat Jehanne himself for her impertinence.

Uncle Durand brought us the news and threw his hands up in despair. He had done all he could. Perhaps Jehanne should return home. Jehanne simply said, 'No. We ask again.'

So, when Uncle Durand returned to his fields, Jehanne and I went alone to the castle.

What fools we were. Innocent, hopeful fools. Two plain country girls, dressed in our red skirts like every other peasant girl in the town, with brown faces and rough hands. Who were we, presuming to call on the sire? We must have seemed like grubs from the soil. What bare-faced nerve, what arrogance! The townsfolk stared at us and one or two covered their noses against what they called our 'foul odour'. But we ignored their insults and knocked long and loud on the castle door. We tried shouting, then using our fists, then banging with a heavy stick. No response. Not a glimmer. And it went on like that for six days.

On the seventh day, there was a change. From the windows high up in the keep, which had so far remained blank, de Baudricourt's men now leaned to look down at us. It seemed that our noise had interrupted their breakfast.

Mouths tore at meat like ravening wolves, fists wiped away grease, faces sank into upturned jugs as if to drown in wine. One man poured out a stream of dregs, but I managed to pull Jehanne out of its way. The wine splashed over my neck and shoulders and I growled at him and shook my fist, vowing, that if I got the chance, I would make him pay for the insult.

At their lewd gestures, I fairly danced with rage, but Jehanne sank to her knees in the middle of the street and began to pray. And, as always, the stillness she had inside seemed, slowly, secretly, to spread out and cover everything. Sounds died away, movements came to rest, the sunlight touched her like a blessing as she knelt there, letting people, animals, wagons pass round her, showering her with dust. And, finally, even de Baudricourt's men fell silent.

I was on the point of pulling her to her feet before the catcalls started again, when the impossible happened. The castle door swung open and we were admitted, ushered up the stairs of a round tower into a solar, where de

Baudricourt's men were now busy seating themselves back at a refectory table, to finish their meal.

But the miracle ended there. If Jehanne's prayer had got us inside, God now took back His help. Standing to endure the men's sniggers, we were on our own.

As far as they were concerned we were ripe entertainment. Two peasant girls, not even local, not under male protection, so, in their eyes, defenceless as new-born babes, demanded to speak to the regional commander. What a joke! I could imagine them calling for us to be admitted: 'Let them in! Let's make them squirm!'

It was a vast and echoing stone room, cold and grey. The long table stretched down the middle and most of the men sat on its far side.

Jehanne and I were not invited to sit: we had to stand facing de Baudricourt and his men, as if we were accused and they were the justices. I burned with anger but held myself tight, knowing that if I cried out, my roars would merely brand me a half-wit. I balled my fists in my shawl, hanging on to Polly, who was snuggled up in its folds. She kicked uneasily, reminding me to let her sit more comfortably.

At first no one spoke to us, but the men gawped and guffawed as if we were comical pictures to examine thoroughly in every last detail, not real people at all.

The floor was littered with greasy bones and dogs quietly chewing on them; the table with the remains of breakfast—a gooseberry tart, apples, cheeses, wine, meat. And in the middle of the men on a more elaborately carved and gilded chair, sat the man I took to be the Sire de Baudricourt, lording it like a king in a palace.

As soon as I saw him I knew what his answer to Jehanne's request would be. Her mission would die here, now, in this room. How could she crown a king and fight the English? Why should he back her? He could have us thrown into a dungeon. Or, if Jehanne mentioned her voices, he could have her certified mad. Frantically, my thoughts picked at a means of escape, but the windows were high above the ground and there were guards either side of the doors.

I looked at each man in turn, defiantly holding their eyes as long as I dared, and tucked Polly close under my shawl, wishing now that I'd left her with Uncle Durand. At least with breakfast more or less over, the men would not be looking for fresh meat, so for the time being Polly was safe.

But I was seen.

'What have you there, *ma belle*?' asked one of de Baudricourt's men.

Red-faced, I couldn't help a growl, and to draw attention away from me, Jehanne took Polly into her cloak and answered the question.

'A hen, my lord, a pet, a travelling companion.'

The room erupted with loud laughter and the man went on, 'Give me the hen: I'll travel with you, pretty one!'

With a wry smile, Jehanne said, 'I'm hardly pretty, my lord, so please do not say so. It sounds like cheap flattery.'

The men burst out laughing again and there were jeers and cries of, 'Well rebuked!', 'This one's a fighter, Guilbert!', 'She'll teach you some manners!'

'Let's see this hen,' said one. 'Why do you carry it? Is it valuable?' said another. 'Does it do tricks?' Someone asked.

'No tricks, lord,' she said. 'But she is valuable to us, the best layer this side of Reims.'

'What, even in winter?'

'If the sky is bright, Polly will lay,' she said, gently producing her from the folds of her cloak and holding her up for them to see.

'A phenomenon,' said one of the men. 'We haven't had fresh eggs for weeks. May I examine this Polly paragon?'

I glanced at Jehanne, but she nodded reassuringly and, with a quaking heart, I watched her pass Polly over. But Polly made up her own mind. When the first man made a rough grab for her, as if to wring her neck then and there, she squawked and flew out of his grasp, then pecked the fingers of anyone who tried to catch her and rushed headlong down the table, causing the dogs who had been lying quietly on and over the men's feet to rouse up and bark, and snap at her little jumps.

Quickly I strode to the end of the table and picked up my hen, smoothing her startled feathers.

'Treat her with care,' Jehanne said to the man. 'She pecks because she's afraid.'

'Treat her with care, Gervaise,' said one of his companions, sniggering.

'Balderdocks,' said Gervaise, sucking his wounded fingers.

'Could she teach my hens to lay?'

The voice was deep and rich. The Sire de Baudricourt was leaning forward and sounded genuinely interested in the answer.

'Do they not know how, my lord?'

'Apparently not. We haven't had eggs for weeks. I should

be grateful for fresh eggs. Is the hen yours?' He swung round to address me. 'Will you lend her to us?'

I opened my mouth but made no sound and he swung back to Jehanne.

'Does she not speak?'

'No, my lord.'

'But she has all her wits?'

'Oh yes. God took her voice when her mother was killed by the English. We pray that He will restore it one day, perhaps when we finally defeat the English and drive them from every corner of France.'

The room fell silent at Jehanne's strong certain voice. The Sire de Baudricourt got to his feet.

'That sounds like a complaint. Are you reminding us of our duty? Take care not to meddle in things you don't understand.'

'What I understand, my lord, is that you sit here at your breakfast while the English steal our land.'

At this the two guards either side of the door stepped forward, grasped her arms and I waited for the inevitable order to throw us into the gutter, but before de Baudricourt could speak, Jehanne called out.

'I am Jehanne of Domrémy, my lord. In God's name, let me speak.'

'So you're Jehanne? Durand Lassois told me you would come.' De Baudricourt gestured to the two guards to stand down. 'I told him to beat you.'

Jehanne met his stare without flinching.

'From Domrémy?' de Baudricourt went on. 'I know your father, Jacques, do I not?'

'Jacques d'Arc's daughter,'—one of his men leaned over

to whisper in his ear—'the young lady who went to the law court rather than marry.'

He leaned back, folding his arms, at ease again. 'What went wrong, Jehanne?' He looked round at his men, inviting them to enjoy the joke. 'Was the man not to your taste? You can't afford to be choosy.' On cue, the room erupted with laughter.

Jehanne straightened her back and lifted her chin. I groaned: one girl against a roomful of professional soldiers. This would end badly.

But I was wrong. She was more than a match for de Baudricourt.

'Robert,' she said, in her clear ringing voice. Robert. It was a bold move to use his first name, and there was a flutter of comments from his men.

'Let her speak,' snapped de Baudricourt, with sudden interest. The room fell instantly silent.

'Robert,' went on Jehanne. 'You and I, being strangers to beauty—' There was a hiss of amazement at that, but again de Baudricourt silenced the room. '—both know it holds little value. The face is an outward show that can deceive. What counts is the heart. Is your heart big enough to hear a message from God?'

'Say on,' said de Baudricourt, in a voice low and dangerous and, as he leant back, I realized that he let her speak only to walk to her own ruin.

'Then hear me, all of you. I have come from God to warn you to get ready.'

Again the hiss and the irritated call for silence.

'Ready for what?' Quiet voice, menacing.

'Ready for the final battle for France. God sends me to

Chinon to speak to the dauphin. I am to lead his army and take him to Reims to be crowned, as his father before him. All France will unite again under his rule.'

There was uproar. Some of the men jumped to their feet and let loose a gale of laughter. One man, playing to the crowd, pretended to fall off the bench with hilarity and rolled on the floor clutching his stomach.

'The dauphin Cha-a-arles?' drawled de Baudricourt. What a world of scorn was in those words. Poor dauphin, the butt of so many jokes. King Charles's illegitimate son, weak-willed and dithering, not a brave man, not the obvious choice for the next king. As I had known it to be, Jehanne's mission was doomed.

De Baudricourt waited for Jehanne to speak, but she stayed silent.

'So, you are to lead the army,' he said finally. 'Hm. Can you fight? What weapon do you favour? Who taught you horsemanship? Are you skilled with a lance? Have you ever faced an enemy in single combat? Can you fight with a sword? Can you even lift one?'

The man called Gervaise, who had been sitting at de Baudricourt's side, got up and rushed round the table. 'Let me! Please! Please!' He drew his sword and someone passed him a second, which he threw to Jehanne. I caught my breath in terror, but she caught the sword by the hilt, planted its point in the floor, and stood calmly with both hands on the pommel. The soldier made his sword dance round her head, beating the air, but she didn't flinch even though the keen blade swished just past her ears, a hair's breadth away.

'Defend yourself,' de Baudricourt urged. 'If you're to get to Chinon, you may well have to.'

'It is not yet time for me to fight,' she said, deftly stepping aside as the man lunged at her, and pushing his shoulder so that he spun away and his swordstroke passed harmlessly by, striking the empty air. Loud laughter and cries of, '*Bravo, la paysanne*!' and '*En avant*, Gervaise!'

Caught off balance the man stumbled, then angrily sprang up, ready to lunge again, but his comrades pulled him back.

'God grant me the skill and the courage to fight when my hour comes.'

In the moment of surprised silence won by this comment, Jehanne placed the sword carefully on the table then walked over to a lectern next to the fireplace, where a map, similar to the one she and Pierre had pored over, was on display. Jehanne studied it, getting her bearings, then stabbed it with her finger. 'The main English forces are here and here. Tell me, Robert, why you are not in the field?'

De Baudricourt marched angrily to join her and the two of them stood facing each other, on either side of the map. They spoke together, firing words at each other like cannons.

'Who sent you?'

'Why do you sit here idle while the English eat away at France like a disease?'

'Who sent you?' The repeated words were a cold challenge.

'One day we shall find ourselves English serfs, not free French any more.'

De Baudricourt's chief men-at-arms were moving round the table to get to her.

'Why are you here?'

As the men laid hands on her, Jehanne said, quietly, as if to persuade a child, 'I come from God. It is God who has sent me.'

The hairs on the back of my neck stood up as I felt again the power of her words. Her passion, her energy shone from her like sunlight. Could de Baudricourt feel it? Perhaps he could because, against the odds, he signalled to his men and they stepped back.

'What do you want?' he said.

'You must write to the dauphin and tell him to listen to me. I shall need an escort, six men will do, for the journey to Chinon.'

'This is foolishness, girl. Go back to your father.'

'I would go home at once, if I could. Do you think I wanted to kneel at your door begging to be let in? By God's will, Robert, I have a holy destiny, and neither you nor I, nor any man or woman alive on God's earth, can stop it.'

De Baudricourt's eyes bored into hers.

'I didn't choose this,' she said.

'If this is a trick, you will pay the price.'

'If this was a trick I would ask for more, wouldn't I? I have stood at your door for six days. I'm hungry and dirty and tired—we both are—but I haven't asked you for food or fresh clothing or even a chair to sit on.'

'God says you must crown the dauphin?' he said, with disbelief.

'The message is clear.'

'Not good enough.'

The room rang with the men's laughter.

'That fool a king?' burst out one of the lords.

'Laugh, lords, if you will,' Jehanne said loudly. 'But hear this. The Dauphin Charles carries royal blood in his veins. To be crowned our king is his destiny. It is my destiny to fight for him, to make him a king and to strengthen his backbone into a rod of steel that will bend to no man.'

A long silence followed this speech, then the men erupted into shouts and guffaws.

'And how do you propose to do that?' said de Baudricourt, calling above the noise.

'I don't know yet. God will tell me what to do.'

'Ha!' De Baudricourt laughed himself at this and turned to his men. 'Send for a physician,' he called. 'Her wits have turned.'

His audience roared their approval.

'Robert!' The urgency in Jehanne's tone stopped de Baudricourt's laughter. 'This is God's work! Not mine. Not yours. God's work! Do you defy Him? For His sake, listen to me!'

De Baudricourt's eyes were like stones.

'Listen to me.' Jehanne's voice was now low and re-assuring.

Was the sire beginning to take her seriously? The lines of his face softened and when his men started to shift and mutter in the uneasy silence, he signalled them to be quiet.

'I do not defy God,' he said. 'No one dare say so. I am His faithful servant.' Jehanne bowed her head in acknowl-edgement. 'Speak, maid. I'm listening.'

'When I walked in here,' Jehanne began, 'you thought I would provide a pleasant hour's entertainment for you and your men. Well, the hour's over, so why haven't you

❖ 51 ❖

ordered my arrest? Why is that, do you think? Is it because in your heart of hearts you know that I might be telling the truth?

'You're a good man, Robert. Let God speak to you. Isn't He telling you to help me? Whether you like it or not, whether you believe it or not, I have to go to the dauphin. God has called me to do this and I cannot refuse, though it costs me everything.'

De Baudricourt sat down in his chair, seemingly at his ease, one hand grasping the lion's head at the end of the chair arm, the other supporting his chin. But his black eyes bored into Jehanne's like an auger.

'Chinon and then Reims?'

Jehanne nodded.

'You'll never succeed.'

'I have to try.'

'Even if you crown the dauphin, you'll need many more soldiers than we presently have to defeat the English. Where will you find them? The French man-in-the-street is nothing but a lazy peasant who thinks only of his belly. He doesn't care who's in charge as long as the wine keeps flowing. You can't trust him to fight.'

'You underestimate your own people. They appear lazy because they lack direction. Who will tell them what to do? The English hold the rivers and the wells, they control the fields and the crops. The people eat or starve according to the whim of the English. They have learned to be helpless. Now they must learn to fight or be for ever slaves. They must have a leader. The one who should lead them skulks in his castle at Chinon like a scolded schoolboy, attacked and undermined by his own captains. But the dauphin is no schoolboy. By law and tradition, he is God's chosen sovereign in France. And I am sent to crown him at Reims. I must get to Chinon. Help me.

'Sire de Baudricourt, God's deputy here in Lorraine, help me. I will not go back to Domrémy.'

From the far end of the table one of the older lords got to his feet and made his way round the others to come close.

'Did you say Domrémy?' he said to Jehanne, bending forward keenly to hear her answer.

'Yes.'

'And you're unmarried?'

'Yes.'

'*Dieu*,' he whispered, shrinking back. His fingers tapped at his lips.

'What is it, Lacroix?' murmured de Baudricourt.

'A old legend, liege, an old story, something made up to entertain children, I thought, but stranger things have happened and been proved true.'

'What story?'

'That France will be saved by a Maid from Lorraine.'

'I am she. I am the Maid,' said Jehanne.

Her voice rang out like a bell and my spine tingled.

'I am the Maid of Lorraine,' she repeated. 'And I need your help.'

Everyone waited in silence for de Baudricourt to make his decision and I knew that we stood at a vital threshold. De Baudricourt's men watched him, ready to follow wherever he led.

'Come back tomorrow,' he said. 'You won't have to wait at the door.'

CHAPTER SIX
DE BAUDRICOURT'S CHALLENGE

The next day we were knocking at the castle door early, when the only other people about in the rosy half-light, were street sellers and tradespeople laying out their wares.

Jehanne's face wore a hard, determined look. Lines of anxiety furrowed her forehead and her lips were drawn tight. To lighten the waiting, I tilted my head and pressed my hands to my cheek, signing that the watchman, who should have opened the door by now, must be asleep, but she didn't smile.

'Asleep?' she said. 'He's no business to be asleep. I have to get on. Time's running out!' Then, just as she finished speaking, the door was opened by the watchman, an old man with slow and deliberate movements, who then beckoned us inside.

We were led past the stairs we had used before, across an inner courtyard, through a tunnel in the rear rampart, and out into a field at the back of the castle. Perhaps Jehanne's words the previous day had had some effect: in all corners of the field, de Baudricourt's men were going through their paces, jumping to the barked commands of a master-at-arms lunging at each other with swords, parrying blows, in preparation for battle practice. From the look of their gear—plates of armour, shields, lances, and swords, and their horses, some grazing, some tossing their heads—I saw that they were all knights, chevaliers, who would ride into battle ahead of the foot soldiers, to break open the enemy lines and drive a path through them. These men were the best fighters, the most skilful, the strongest. So many French chevaliers like my father had sacrificed their lives at Agincourt, through English treachery.

Grandmère had told me about the tournaments, so I knew what was involved when two warriors met in the lists, long fenced-off tracks of the field where the knights practised charging each other on horseback, lances at the ready. I had seen images too of the quintain, and the archery targets. But nothing prepared me for the scene before me now, the real thing.

Soldiers are loud and fierce. They move with quick, strong movements. They are tough and thick-skinned. There's nothing gentle about them. This was a dangerous place.

'Wait here,' said the watchman, showing us to a bench. I sat down at once, trembling with fear, wringing my hands, but Jehanne stood, calm and still, her arms folded.

'So, we're to be kept waiting again,' she said.

A trumpet sounded and I jumped up to stand with her, watching as two knights in full armour took their positions at either end of the field and prepared to race down it towards their collision. A red and white flag fluttered to the ground to signal the start and the knights pricked their horses into a gallop and thundered forward. My heart pounded. The noise was terrifying. I focused on one of the knights, the one coming towards us. His head was down, his lance poised. What would it be like to face him?

Craaaaasshhh! The two riders met, their lances clashed, and they rode on, my knight unbowed, but his opponent swaying in his saddle like a broken doll amid wild cheering and shouts from the grooms and squires who stood on the sidelines. My knight swerved to a halt at the bottom of the field, passed his lance to his squire, and leaned down to pat his horse's neck.

'*Bien fait, mon héros!*' he called. His breath and his horse's breath mingled like clouds around their heads. Then he sat upright again as another opponent took the field.

It was dangerous but exhilarating and I was eager to watch. Then I heard Jehanne say, 'Good morning, sire. I've come for your answer. Do I have your support?'

As the second round of the trials began and the knights thundered headlong down the lists again, de Baudricourt followed the contest, deliberately keeping her waiting. When the crash came and my knight's opponent was unseated, he walked away from us and shouted angrily to the man on the ground,

'Wake up, Bernard!' and he gestured to Bernard's squire, who promptly threw a pail of water over his master's head.

De Baudricourt turned on his heel and came back to us.

Jehanne pressed him for an answer. 'I need a letter giving your recommendation to the dauphin. I need an escort of armed men. I must leave soon.'

'Jehanne d'Arc,' he said, 'I'm well aware of what you need to gain an audience with the dauphin. But are you aware of what your mission involves? Look at yourself. Forgive me, but you don't look like a warrior, yet you ask me to approach the dauphin and recommend you.'

As the third pair of knights thundered down the lists, he said, 'Do you really think you're up to leading an army?'

Craaassh! The knights met and parted.

'Jehanne. Could you do what they do?'

Panic rocked me as I realized what he was asking.

Jehanne clenched her hands behind her back until the knuckles showed white. 'If I must,' she answered defiantly.

'If? Of course you must, girl, if you're to lead an army! What did you imagine it would involve? Cheering them on from the sidelines? Bathing their hurts with vinegar water? Patting their hands and telling them everything would be different after a good night's sleep?'

De Baudricourt turned his back on her, then strode to the barrier.

'Look at them, Jehanne. Look hard. If my men believe in you and this mission, they will risk their lives. They will die for you.'

'Not for me, sire, but for God.'

De Baudricourt paused and then said, 'I admit that crowning the next king is essential. You're right, maid. France has been without a king for too long. It would be a strategic victory as great as winning a battle and send a clear signal to the English that the war is far from over.'

'And to our own people.'

'True.' He turned round to face her. 'Some of these men believe you already. They think that you are the Maid of Lorraine. They believe you really can turn the tide in our favour. But—' De Baudricourt stabbed his finger at her. 'Hear this, maid. If I support you—no, no, I said "if"—I must be certain that you will never let any of these warriors down. And I tell you, if any one of them dies, or is injured, if any one of them comes to the slightest harm because you have faltered at the critical hour, I will find you and kill you.'

Jehanne blanched at this, but she kept her eyes on him, meeting de Baudricourt's angry stare.

'Milord,' called a groom, drawing away his attention. He walked up, leading a great black horse. Over its back was draped a chain-mail shirt, and other pieces of armour, greaves and a breastplate, strapped to the saddle. The groom carried a lance and a silver helmet.

'Jehanne, put it on.' De Baudricourt made the request very quietly, and there we stood, at a crossroads, as he presented Jehanne with the challenge . . . *Could you do as they do?*

I was paralysed with fear. Why hadn't we foreseen this? This was where the whole thing came to an end.

The groom began to shift the armour from the back of the horse, and my mouth dropped open with shock as I saw Jehanne take the reins and swing herself up into the saddle, neatly tucking up her skirt so that she could sit comfortably astride, with the high war saddle holding her firmly back and front.

The groom climbed a mounting block to hand her a breastplate and helmet but Jehanne said, 'No, thank you, I don't need any armour. God will protect me. Hand me the lance.'

There was a look of surprise and grudging respect on de Baudricourt's face as the groom passed her the lance. 'Have you done this before, maid?' he said, straightening her boot in the stirrup.

'No, sire.'

'Some advice, then,' he said, going forward to hold the reins. 'Find the point of balance on the lance, then hold it lightly and let the speed of your horse drive it home. Keep that arm supple: if it's stiff and unbending, the shock of collision will break it. Like this, yes, that's better.' He handed her the reins and stepped back, then said, half smiling, 'Well, I admire your courage, maid. God be with you.'

Jehanne spurred her horse to the start of the course. I hardly dared look, then scolded myself for a coward and took my hands away from my eyes.

Jehanne sat bolt upright in the saddle and held her lance steady. I felt again that stillness of hers and saw that her horse stood quite still, as well, as if aware of the immensity of the challenge. De Baudricourt signalled his men to stand back. The whole company gathered in silence to watch Jehanne ride the list.

She looked straight ahead down the field. The other rider waited, the trumpet sounded, the flag dropped, and Jehanne touched the sides of her horse, once, with a powerful kick. Like the destrier he was he thundered forward, nostrils flaring. His ears flicked back as Jehanne leaned slightly forward to take aim.

Craaaasssh! The two riders met in a cloud of dust and I craned my neck to see who had survived.

Thank God! Both had stayed in their saddles. At the top of the course, Jehanne threw down her lance and came riding back to us, her long hair tousled and streaming free in the wind. With a wild cry and a wave I ran to meet her and she reached down to touch my hand. Then she rode over to her opponent. When the knight took off his helmet, unhurt, her face glowed bright with success. *You were born for this*, I thought. *You were!* And that was when I first thought that it all might be possible.

'Well done, Jehanne,' called de Baudricourt, as his groom held the black horse and Jehanne dismounted. He was delighted with her performance, but all Jehanne said was, 'Now give me an escort to Chinon.'

De Baudricourt laughed. 'Perhaps.'

'What else must I do?' Her voice was as sharp as a blade.

'You must be aware of the rumours.'

'What rumours?'

'Honest fears that you must dispel before anyone takes your part.'

'What fears?'

'Let's go inside. Have you breakfasted?'

'What fears, milord?'

Refusing to answer, de Baudricourt strode ahead of us into the castle.

CHAPTER SEVEN
THE VOICE OF THE PEOPLE

'What fears, milord?'

We scampered up the stairs, close on de Baudricourt's heels. More affected by the challenge than I had thought, Jehanne spoke in a high, sharp voice and her breath came in quick gasps, as she pestered him for an answer.

But de Baudricourt would not explain until he had eaten his meal.

'Eat your fill,' he said, gesturing to the full platters on the table. I picked up a piece of cooked rabbit and a chunk of bread, and offered some to Jehanne, but she shook her head and would accept only water.

We sat next to each other in a quiet corner of the room. I pushed some bread at her, but again she refused it.

'I think I would choke,' she said.

De Baudricourt, in between bites, was speaking to the master-at-arms, the first to come in from the field. He was quickly followed by the men, who entered in twos and threes, all talking loudly about the challenge and about Jehanne. When they saw her sitting there, they fell quiet and nodded or looked at her gravely. The younger ones stared, as if she had grown two heads, then flushed when I stared back. Jehanne, looking pensively into the fire, ignored them all.

After his meal, de Baudricourt called the room to attention. 'Gentlemen, you all witnessed an act of great courage this morning, from this young woman who sits there as quietly as a mouse—'a ripple of laughter—'a mouse with the heart of a lion'—a roar of approval. He waited for the noise to die back, then went on, 'You know why she is here. Now, what should I do? Should I send her to the dauphin?'

There were ready shouts of 'Why not? Where's the harm?'

De Baudricourt seized on these words. 'Where's the harm, indeed? Is there harm in Jehanne d'Arc? Forgive me, Jehanne, but some say there might be, for all we know. Sometimes the Devil has an innocent face.'

'No!' said Jehanne, standing up. 'I—'

De Baudricourt cut across her words: 'These are the fears of honest men, and if you can't convince them to follow you, your mission ends here.'

Jehanne moved to the centre of the room and the men gathered in groups to surround her.

'What are these fears?' she said in a clear voice. 'Explain, milord.'

De Baudricourt regarded the circle of men, then turned to face her.

'It's said you're a witch.'

Jehanne gave a shocked laugh then, gathering herself, she took a deep breath and clasped her hands in front of her.

'God has sent me, Robert.'

'Then He will forgive me if I ask you to go through one more test, for the sake of these honest men.'

'Yes,' she said.

'After this, you will have my decision.'

'God is patient, even if I am not,' Jehanne replied.

With a frown, de Baudricourt beckoned forward a man who sat alone at the end of the room, cloaked and hooded, all in black.

As the circle of men parted to let him through and he stood in front of Jehanne and threw back his hood, I shoved my way forward and fell to my knees, bowing my head for his blessing. It was my priest from Reims, our family confessor, Father Cornelius.

'I'm glad to see you again, Mariane,' he said, laying his hand on my head. 'God bless you, child.'

I looked up at him. *What brought him to Vaucouleurs? How long had he been here? Why had he not sought me out?*

My questions were soon forgotten as, for the first time in months, my heart flooded with real happiness and tears pricked my eyes. Here was a link with home. It was good to see him again.

'Proceed, Father,' said de Baudricourt and Father Cornelius's gaze passed from me to Jehanne. In the silence that had settled on the room, he made the sign of the cross in the air between himself and Jehanne, as if establishing a barrier. As he did so, he called in a loud voice:

'Spirit within, I command you, in the name of Our Lord, Jesus Christ, show yourself.'

The company gasped as Jehanne seemed to collapse to her knees. Some of them drew back and grasped their swords, as if they expected a demon to appear any minute.

I started forward to help her, but then she seemed to recover and gently pushed away my hand. She didn't look up but stayed kneeling, breathing deeply, her head bowed to her chest, hands pressed together, as if she were praying.

Father Cornelius tried again.

'Spirit within, I conjure you, in the name of our Lord, reveal yourself. Speak!'

At this Jehanne looked up and fixed her eyes on him, but she still made no sound.

Holding her gaze, Father Cornelius lifted up the silver crucifix he wore on his chest and shouted as if to bring down the castle walls:

'Demon, depart! Go back to the infernal regions from whence you have come! Leave this place!'

Again there was a pause, but Jehanne made no movement or sound. Father Cornelius spoke once more:

'Jehanne D'Arc, if you are truly inspired by the Holy Spirit, and not possessed by a demon from hell, then approach and kiss this crucifix, the sign of God's power on earth.'

There was a silence for several minutes. I held my breath, my eyes fixed on Jehanne as, still on her knees, she shuffled slowly towards Father Cornelius until she was near enough to reach up to the cross. With shaking fingers she pressed it once to her lips, to her forehead, then let it go, and as Father Cornelius was stepping back, caught the hem of his robe and kissed that.

Then she said, 'If ever there be any evil thing within me, let me die. Stop my breath here and now if I am misled in my mission by Satan, the father of lies. Stop my heart, shrivel my immortal soul, if my quest is not by God's design, but a plan of the Devil.'

We all waited again, but as the minutes crept by, still she knelt there, living, breathing, praying.

Father Cornelius reached down and picked her up, gently kissing the top of her head.

'Bless you, my child, in the name of the Father.' The rest of his blessing was lost in the roar of shouts that greeted Jehanne's success. A knight standing next to the window cried out: 'Sire, look!' and gestured to the market place below. We all crowded to the windows, leant over the stone sills, and looked down.

The air was still. Pale sunlight washed over the damp tiles on the neighbouring roofs. Pigeons flew up or sat nestling, croo-crooing softly on the ledges.

A large, silent crowd looked up at us. A murmur ran through it when they saw Jehanne. As if to a signal, still silent, they began to fall to their knees with clasped hands, their upturned faces fixed on hers.

'There seems to be some interest in your quest, Jehanne,' de Baudricourt said.

I scanned the crowd and recognized Uncle Durand. Was this his doing? He's a good man. For a few minutes the two parties stared at each other: the liege lord and military commander, and the common people of France.

The voice of the people was clear. *Let her go. What have you to lose? We need something to believe in. She says she's from God—perhaps she is. Let her try.*

De Baudricourt's men now surrounded her, cheering her on, claiming her as theirs. And I stood back and watched, seeing that she was the catalyst they were waiting for, the key that would unlock the door of their determination to win France for the French. Later that morning I was about to follow Jehanne down the spiral steps, bursting to communicate with her, when Father Cornelius called me from behind. He beckoned me back into the room.

'God moves in mysterious ways, Mariane,' he said. 'I was on my way to find you. I would have left for Domrémy later today. But there's no need, because here you are!' He took my hands in his and sat me down next to him on a bench by the fire.

'Your cousin Jehanne has stirred things up, hasn't she? That was a brave display she gave this morning. I was almost convinced myself. Poor soul, she is—' He tapped his head, '—a little brainsick, no? She needs the doctor, not the dauphin. I wonder why the sire is so patient?'

I took my hands from his.

'I'm sorry to upset you, Mariane. You must beware of false prophets. I have seen many so-called "saints" on my travels: the mad, the deluded, who make similar claims. But—' He shrugged, '—they are usually harmless and sometimes it's better to let the people have their fantasies for a while. They never last long, but fizzle out in the cold light of the real world. In these grim times, Jehanne's adventures will provide entertainment.'

I stood up.

'Do you really think she will be allowed to speak to the dauphin? Mariane—you must leave Jehanne to her dreams; you have tasks of your own. Are you not wondering why I set out to find you?'

There was a long pause, then I clapped my hand to my mouth. *Grandmère*.

Father Cornelius said gently, 'I'm afraid Grandmère Alys is dying.'

CHAPTER EIGHT
MY INHERITANCE

'Don't worry about Polly, I'll take good care of her!' Jehanne called, as I set off for Reims with Father Cornelius. Tears sprang to my eyes as I gave up my pet. It felt as if part of my life was over.

As Father Cornelius and I threaded our way through the market place, I wondered how the sun could shine, when grandmère was mortally ill. My spirit fled to her.

When we rode into the yard, a week later, I fell out of my saddle and ran straight into the cottage. Grandmère lay in her bed, which had been moved next to the fire, with a clear view of the door. Her face was thin and as white as bone, her hair like mist; but her eyes blazed when she saw me.

'I've been waiting for you,' she said, in a rasping voice. 'You left Domrémy?' It was a complaint and a question and I grasped her hand, struggling to speak, furious with myself for not being able to explain.

'You want to tell your grandmother about Jehanne?' said Father Cornelius.

Please, please. I nodded.

'She knows,' he said, setting out wafer and wine.

'Jehanne. Stay with her,' grandmère whispered, gripping my hand. Puzzled, I hesitated. 'Promise. Stay with her,' she repeated. So I nodded and, reassured, she sank back into her pillows and rested silent for a few minutes. Gently I massaged her hand, as I used to when the cold weather bit into her joints. What in the world would I do without her?

After a few minutes, she opened her eyes and raised herself, pointing to the key on its cord round my neck.

'Fetch the box.' She was having difficulty breathing. 'The box . . . Mariane. It's what the key is for, what the soldiers who killed your mother wanted . . . the box contains your inheritance.'

Father Cornelius stood guard while I went outside. With my back to the well, I faced west. Forward a hundred paces. East, thirty. North, forty—directions my mother had made me learn as a child. The box contained my father's things! I had never seen it or its contents, but now my mother was dead, I supposed it was mine.

I couldn't help a thrill of excitement. My father was a nobleman, one of the royal chevaliers. The box had come to my mother after his death. She had buried it, I don't know why—too many painful memories perhaps—but she had kept the key. What if it held treasure, gold or jewels? I would be rich.

My joy died when I thought of grandmère. Passing on the box meant only one thing: that she knew she was dying. My anxious mind made the decisions: if there were treasure in the box, I would use it to buy medicine and treatment from the finest doctors in Paris. I would spend every last sou to save her life.

I dug in the spot marked by a boulder and was relieved to find, within three hand spans, a large leather sack containing a rectangular wooden box. I ran with it back to the cottage.

Father Cornelius followed me inside and stood with me as I placed the sack carefully by grandmère on the coverlet.

'Take out the box, Mariane,' she whispered.

I unpicked the drawstring of the sack, which was stiff with soil and mould, then took out the box. It was a beautiful object: ebony inlaid with ivory patterns.

'Unlock it.'

I took the key from round my neck and fitted it into the lock. But it wouldn't turn. Grandmère sighed as if the effort of speaking were taking all her strength, so I jumped up and took a smear of goose-fat from the jar and rubbed the key with it, and placed it again in the lock. This time it turned easily and the lid fell back.

My heart was thudding, the blood hot in my cheeks. This was my father's legacy, left for my mother and me. I had never been allowed to see it before. What was it? Gold? Jewels?

A brown cloth covered the box's contents. I removed it and turned to place it on grandmère's table. Underneath were two mouldy shapes.

'They are yours, Mariane. Take them.'

With trembling fingers, one by one, I picked up the objects.

There was no gold, no jewels, no parchment conveying land to me. Only, as I saw within minutes, brushing the mildew away, a muddy old glove and a book, a missal, made up of folded pages of vellum, beautifully decorated. There was a scrap of cloth too, a badge torn from a soldier's tunic.

Grandmère took the badge and stretched it out between

quivering fingers for me to see. Two blue chevrons on a white roundel, smeared with mud.

'This is it, Mariane. Your inheritance. From your father.' I took the badge. Was this the device of my father's family? His name was François de Louvier. Was this the de Louvier crest? I put it to one side and picked up the missal, then put that down and picked up my father's glove. Was this all? Was there no treasure?

'Your father was—' Her voice was a wisp of sound, almost too faint to hear.

I waited for her to go on, but she had fallen into a light sleep.

I turned the glove over and some of the mud flaked off, revealing the stiff leather beneath, still bent to the shape of his hand.

I never knew my father: he had died a hero of Agincourt, six days after the battle, on the day I was born. My mother and he never married. She told me the story of how he had led the charge at the English archers, and had been cut down by an English arrow. Father Cornelius had found him alive and had taken him home, to an estate called La Paix. Then when he died, Father Cornelius had brought his things to my mother. And she had buried them.

Handling his badge made me feel very close to maman and tears welled up in my eyes.

'He loved your mother, Mariane, and he loved France,' grandmère whispered.

She lingered for another ten deep but she never spoke again. As she sank lower and lower, slow breath by slow breath, I watched over her and waited and prayed. And then the time came when I knew she was gone. There was no pain, hers was an easy death, and I thanked God for it, as Father Cornelius and I said our final prayers over her body.

Then I too must have slept and, woken by some sixth sense, opened my eyes to semi-darkness.

I was alone. A solitary candle flickered in a draught at the head of grandmère's bed. Her body was cold and white like marble. I listened for any strange sound, but it was peaceful everywhere. What danger had woken me? I searched the shadows, but saw nothing. I got up and, taking the candle, looked in the back room and round the buttery door for Father Cornelius. He had gone. And so had the box.

I left the cottage and, extinguishing the candle flame, crossed the yard. Bright moonlight lit my way. I tried to call out for Father Cornelius, but only made the usual strangled cries of my dumb throat. I tried to think. Where would he be? Had he taken my box? Then I saw the gleam of light in the church and with a flood of relief ran down the path.

Father Cornelius, fearing another English attack, had probably taken the box to the church for safe keeping. There was a large empty tomb in the crypt, where I knew people often left their valuables. Was that what he was doing, now that the town was empty? There was no one here now, except Father Cornelius and me. Our neighbours had been on the move when we arrived, in the middle of an evacuation.

I opened the door into the church and, with immense relief, saw that the priest was here. Candles burnt in the nave at the far end. The crypt door stood ajar and cast a strip of light across the gravestones set in the chancel floor.

I burst into a run, then, ashamed of my irreverence, forced myself to walk slowly down to the chancel, then stop to bow my head and drop a low courtesy to the tabernacle, before darting to the crypt door.

On the top step I waited, listening. Father Cornelius must be down there, but I couldn't hear a sound. I knocked lightly on the door, but there was no answering call. With a beating heart and cold hands, I walked down the winding steps.

Father Cornelius was there and had already opened the tomb. My box was set on the lid and other valuables were there too, laid out on an old altar cloth. He looked up as I entered the crypt, then said, 'Close the door,' and I did so. 'Your box, Mariane,' he said, 'here for safe keeping.' I smiled my thanks and relief, but as I reached for the box, he snatched it up and tipped out the contents, so that they tumbled out in a heap. I bit my lip, thinking it a shame to treat my father's things in such a way. Even if they weren't valuable, they were precious to me.

I reached for the glove, but he picked it up and examined it, then threw it down, scattering flakes of mud on his cassock. He seemed angry. Shocked and bewildered, I retrieved the glove, and placed it behind me on a stone ledge projecting from the rear wall of the crypt. Trying to stay calm, I went to him. Perhaps I could find out what the trouble was. Perhaps I could help. I laid my hand on his arm but, as if my touch burnt him, he gasped and threw me off and I stumbled backwards and fell, knocking my hip against the corner of the tomb.

Rubbing my injury, I leaned against the wall, my eyes wide with confusion. My priest, my confessor, my mentor, had suddenly become a monster. I shook my head slowly, my eyes glued to him. Was he mad?

Father Cornelius shook out the pages of the missal. With distaste he threw them to the ground. When they fell at my feet, I slipped down the wall, gathered them together, and put them with the glove. I moved carefully so as not to provoke him.

'It's not here,' he said, screwing up the badge and throwing it over my head into a dark corner of the crypt. 'So where is it? Someone's made a mistake. It's a pity those fools killed your mother, instead of persuading the truth out of her.' He bundled up the valuable items into the cloth. 'I'll take these for my trouble.'

But then he made his mistake because, shoving the bundle nearer the candle so that he could see to knot the corners, he turned his back on me. I darted round the tomb and seized his cloak, and with a supreme effort, yanked him round to face me.

His face was so close to mine that I could smell the stench of his breath, but I roared as loudly as I could, enjoying the look of shock in his eyes, and tried to shake him to the ground.

He was too strong for me. Things might have gone differently if I had brought my quarterstaff, but as it was he was able to shove me back so that I fell again, the breath knocked out of my body.

As he moved to the door I sprang after him, but I was too late. He slipped through and kicked it shut behind him with a resounding clang. 'Goodbye, Mariane. God keep you.'

Through the dense wood of the crypt door, his words

were faint. I hammered on the door and roared and growled, then paused to listen. The only sound I heard was the grating of the key as it turned in the lock.

CHAPTER NINE
DECISIONS

I banged and banged on the door until my hands ached and my wrists shivered with pain, but no one came. There was no one to hear me.

My aunts, Thérèse and Renée, had gone with the others. They knew how poorly grandmère was and they had left her to die alone. I could hardly believe it, but as time went on, the thought knocked at my mind like a cruel spectre. *They left her. They've gone. They're not coming back.*

I'm ashamed to say that I let myself slip down the door and fell, weak, to the ground, my courage ebbing, like wine from a leaky barrel.

The crypt smelt of death: the cold, damp, musty smell of decay. The tombs were ages old, arranged on shelves round the room. The sight and smell of death had never bothered me. I was used to it: the cold flesh, the pale skin, as I helped grandmère and my mother wash the dead and prepare them for burial.

It was the loneliness of it that now left me weak, washing over me in icy waves, leaving me prey to the bone-cold fear that no one would come, no one would find me, and I would die here, alone.

Roaring, I jumped up and banged again on the door, desperate for my aunts, for grandmère and maman, for Jehanne, and finally for God and His Angels to save me.

Then, when I least expected it, God came to me and spoke my name.

'Mariane. Mariane.' I froze, hugging myself with a new terror, that quickly gave way to relief and thanks. My arms dropped from the door. My body breathed again. *Thank you, thank you, Lord*, I said in my mind.

'It's me!' God called. Then: 'Stand away from the door!'

My eyes flew wide as the door burst open. 'Mariane!' I fell forward, into the arms of my aunt Thérèse. My aunt Renée was right behind her.

They had just returned from settling their families at the evacuation site. Father Cornelius had urged them to go, waved them away after we had arrived and I had rushed in to see grandmère. He had promised to fetch them if grandmère got worse. But they were too anxious to stay away and crept back as soon as it was safe to do so. And now they found grandmère dead and me missing. Where was Father Cornelius? Looking for him in the church, they had heard me banging on the crypt door.

Now they began to see the situation for themselves. They looked at the empty tomb.

'Father Cornelius took everything and locked you in?'

I nodded and we spent a few minutes wrapped in a single hug, the three of us, as they struggled to take in all that had happened.

Before we left the crypt, I quickly gathered my father's things and put them back in the box, and when I rejoined my aunts, they exchanged smiles, reassured that at least I had kept my legacy.

My aunts spoke about the treachery of Father Cornelius. They could hardly credit it. Why had he done this? Where was he now? The men might want to leave to track him and the valuables down. Which was worse, losing the valuables or staying to face the English without the men? In between these unanswerable questions, they would break off to cuddle me and talk over my head about what was going to happen to me. For the time being, I'd better go back with them to the camp, but then, when the present danger was over, perhaps I could consider Grandmère Alys's cottage as my own. But there was a silence after they had said this, and a look passed between them, full of meaning; the cottage and land were valuable. They could be sold to replace much that was lost. My aunts looked at me and were torn.

But I had already made my decision about what to do next, and it fell into clear focus when my aunt Renée spoke of me as 'the orphan'. I didn't want to stay here as a burden. I would leave and find my way back to Jehanne.

Days later, after Grandmère's simple burial, when I had had time to recover a little from my grief, I saddled my mother's old horse, Castanier, and rode away from my home at dawn, my breath clouding the February air.

The future was an unknown land. What would I find there? I left in secret, not wanting my aunts' questions and worries to make me falter. My plan, sketchy at best, was to rejoin Jehanne and trust in God for the rest. My hope was weak, my faith in her calling a poor, brittle thing.

Jehanne would be on her way to Chinon by now. What if the dauphin supported her? Her next goal was Orléans. To raise the siege, she must mount an attack on the English. Open war.

Grandmère's words came back to me—'*Stay with her*'— and strengthened my purpose.

A curl of excitement lit through me at the prospect of battle, something waking inside me, raising its head, ready to roar at the feel of a blade.

Meeting the high road, I stopped briefly to look back. I had left like a shadow crossing a sunlit room, but I did leave a message for my aunts on grandmère's table: all her clean linen in neat piles, all her pots and pans, her store of medicines set in orderly rows, all the things I had inherited on her death, that I now left for them to use, and the deed of ownership of the land and the cottage that I found tucked into my grandmother's book. I left it in the most obvious place, where my aunts would be bound to see it, and weighed it down with a piece of slate. It would tell them that I had left for good and that they could do with the cottage what they pleased.

On the slate I chalked a sign to say where I had gone: Jehanne's emblem, the Cross of Lorraine.

I focused on my destination. The road ahead was long and lonely. There was no time to waver, to cry or to grieve. I gave Castanier's flanks a sharp tap and galloped away. To war.

CHAPTER TEN
CHINON

As I rode through the countryside on the long journey to Chinon, the sun rose each morning on dreadful scenes. The land was derelict, fields left unworked, overgrown with thistles and tares, and there were signs of the English everywhere.

At every farm gate English flags flew from stakes thrust into the ground. At every crossroads bodies swung from the gallows, French men and women. Huddles of English soldiers hunkered down nearby, at games of dice, swilling their English ale. At an inn where I thought to take lodging, there were English revellers, playing their tuneless pipes, shouting out in their coarse, ugly language. Seeing my land treated in such a fashion made me see the true meaning of war. How could we live under English conquerors, never to be free French again?

I soon began to avoid villages, heading for open country instead. It made my journey even longer but better my own resources than English 'hospitality'. Water was the first thing to find, to refill my skins, then bread. If Jehanne could survive on a simple diet, so could I.

I looked out for a friendly face, a farmer's wife or householder who wouldn't mind sharing a loaf with a lone traveller. But everywhere was silent. The lanes were deserted and I trotted past empty cottages. Sometimes I saw faces, white and staring, peeping out at me from the shadows then pulling back. These people, afraid to go on with their daily lives, cowered in their homes, like animals threatened by a cunning predator. Resistance meant death. We French had only two choices: to accept the English conquerors or to die. The English oppressors were strong and merciless. It would take a miracle to give us a French victory. I rode on, because there was nothing else I could do.

But perhaps with Jehanne I could do something. Sometimes I think there is a pattern to everything, that our lives hang together like the threads of a spider's web, held in place by the whole design. Ignorant of my birth, I had spent my childhood waiting to be born into my true self, like a moth inside a cocoon. Now I had the chance to be a warrior like my father, to fight for France, riding at Jehanne's side into battle. The more I saw the more I wanted to fight back and, never far from my mind, was my wish for revenge.

After weeks of hard riding, I came within reach of Chinon, and saw, in the distance, a crowd of people, all travelling the road ahead of me. I caught up with them, anxious for news, and found myself in the middle of a carnival, or so it seemed, with men, women, and children, old and young, strong and lame, all singing and dancing, as if victory was already assured.

A priest in black denounced them for behaving so frivolously, but the crowd ignored him and, as he angrily galloped away, they laughed and cheered. So what was the cause for their celebration? As newcomers joined the crowd, I walked alongside and listened to their conversation.

'What's happening? What's this? A carnival?'

'Not exactly,' replied a fat man wearing a red cloak. 'We're following the Maid. The Maid of Lorraine. Yes, she's really here, like the story said. God's sent her to help us. It's a miracle! We're saved. She's going to see the dauphin at Chinon. Why don't you join us?'

My heart leapt to hear this. Jehanne? Had I found her so quickly? I thought she would be with de Baudricourt's escort, not with this crowd.

'Where is this Maid?' asked one of the newcomers. 'Can she heal? I've a terrible bad stomach. I'd like to see her.'

'You and every other Tom, Dick, and Harry! You'll have to stand in the queue, friend. We'll see her tonight. She's promised there'll be a Mass for us at the end of the day. She will be there.'

'Where is she now?'

'Way ahead. She's going to Chinon, I told you, she's going to talk to the dauphin. Hey—' he called as the man moved off, hurrying on down the column, '—you won't be able to see her. She's well guarded.'

I mounted Castanier and spurred him on, passing the man to get to the head of the column. There was now a long gap between the followers—rag, tag, bobtail troop that they were—and the rear of the official escort, whom I recognized from their livery. I stood up in my stirrups to find Jehanne, but saw only de Baudricourt's men-at-arms, wheeling in unison through the gates of Chinon. Where was she? I searched the first few of the followers, but couldn't see her anywhere, and my strength faded. I had come a long, weary way. Perhaps she had ridden on far ahead with her message. Perhaps the dauphin had sent out his own men to escort her and she was with him now.

Vaucouleurs seemed a lifetime away. The Maid. These people were singing about their saviour, the Maid of Lorraine. What right had I to claim her attention? Would she have time for me now? She was no longer Jehanne of Domrémy. She had the ear of the dauphin. Perhaps I would never reach her or see her again.

Heavyhearted, I left the column and rode off across the fields, taking a shortcut to the city gates, ignoring the shouts and songs from the people as they filed towards the city, beating drums and sounding horns as if it were a New Year's Day hunting party.

When I finally entered the gates, I made for the nearest tavern, intending to use my last few coins to buy the services of an ostler for Castanier and lodging for myself, at least for one night. I was lucky. In the inn yard I dismounted and watched the man at the door turning groups of travellers away.

'One! I have room for one—one only!'

I took my father's missal from my pack and stepped forward.

'You're alone? A pilgrim, eh?'

I nodded and held out my coins, then gestured at Castanier.

'Of course,' he said, summoning the ostler. The innkeeper tried to steer me inside the inn, but I held back to see that Castanier was properly stabled and I was reassured when the boy-ostler patted his neck and whispered to him as he led him away. I followed my host inside.

'One for the garret!' he called and, as a tiny servant girl appeared at my side, said, 'Supper's at eight.'

The inn downstairs was packed full and I was glad to find that there were fewer people in the upper rooms. By the time I had reached the foot of the ladder that led up to the garret, the place was empty, the noise of the revellers reduced to a dull drone.

I pushed back my hood and put my foot on the bottom rung, intent on sleeping before supper, when I heard behind me a voice that I recognized. Bertrand de Poulengy, sent by de Baudricourt as part of Jehanne's escort. I had my back to him and, as I whisked round, I glimpsed him disappearing into a room at the far end of the corridor. I sped down to the door and knocked hesitantly.

De Poulengy answered.

'Enfin, c'est toi! Tu est venue!' he said, pulling me into a warm bear-hug. I grinned and submitted to being kissed on both cheeks. Then he stood aside to introduce me to his comrades. There were only two of them, in what was probably the best room in the inn. I took in a big bed, with a mattress and white linen sheets, room enough for half a dozen, let alone three, and a table with two jugs of wine and a large loaf. A fire burnt low on a stone hearth at one end of the room.

'You know de Metz,' said de Poulengy, and I was hugged and kissed a second time.

The third man was engaged in washing himself at a stand with a big basin and ewer. He poured water over his scalp and rubbed it hard, as if he had the itch. As he grabbed a cloth and dried himself, I became aware that de Poulengy and de Metz had moved to the door. *'Au revoir,'*

❖ 85 ❖

they called and I turned, shocked at being left alone with a stranger. 'See you later.' The door opened and closed and they were gone.

When I looked back at their comrade, my heart jolted.

It was Jehanne. Jehanne stood in front of me. She was smiling. I clapped my hand to my mouth. She wore the tunic and high boots of a young man, and her hair had been cut into a boy's short crop. But the eyes and the smile were unmistakable, and I found myself seized and held in a long and powerful embrace. 'Mariane . . . It's so good to see you,' she said.

Laughing and crying together, I held her at arm's length to take in the full effect. 'Mm,' I muttered, raising my eyebrows. Jehanne laughed out loud. 'Mm . . . mm,' I said again, fingering the fine cloth of her grey tunic and shaking my open hand in admiration. Her new clothes were not cheap. 'Uncle Durand supplied them,' she said, hugging me as if I were her long-lost child.

As we ate supper together Jehanne was beside herself with joy. We sat back, sipping our watered wine, warm in the glow of our friendship, and she reached over and tapped my hidden pocket where she knew slate and chalkstone lay, saying, 'Tell me everything that's happened.' Reaching forward I jabbed her chest. 'Yes, I'll tell you everything too,' she said. And I sensed her profound relief that I had found my way back to her.

'Where is Father Cornelius?' Jehanne asked. 'How is your grandmother? Was it as bad as you feared?'

Through signs and drawings and Jehanne's intuitive guesswork, I told my story, about Father Cornelius's treachery, and about my grandmother's death.

'And your inheritance, Mariane? What was it? A pot of gold? Six hundred rubies and a thousand diamonds?'

I shook my head, smiled ruefully, then brought out the box and showed her the contents. Carefully Jehanne picked up each item in turn.

'Your father was a hero, Mariane.' She held the glove reverentially.

'Besmirched with the mud of the battlefield,' she murmured. 'Agincourt. I wonder why he sent it to your mother? It seems too harsh a souvenir.' She looked at me. 'I'm sorry. I shouldn't have said that.'

I pressed her hand to say there was no need for her apology.

Thoughtfully I packed the objects back in the box and hid it again in my pack and Jehanne said, 'Time later to unravel these mysteries when we go home.'

Home? Where was that? I wondered. Could we ever go back? Could anyone? Nothing would be the same, would it? You can't unlearn what you know. The moth can't return to the cocoon.

That night she told me that she had already sent a request to see the dauphin and had received the reply that he might see her within a day or two, if she were still in Chinon. Meanwhile she was to explain herself and her strange mission to members of his council who would interview her the next day.

I poured out more wine and Jehanne sat back in the chair, her legs loose and relaxed, like those of a young squire.

'I'm to be patient, Mariane. Patient. How can I be patient when the English creep everywhere like floodwater? Now these councillors ask exactly why I am here! Are they really such dimwits? I've told them until I'm hoarse that I've come from God—but that's not enough. Ha! The councillors demand to know more. Well, I shall be patience itself and say things simply, so that there's no misunderstanding: I am to raise the siege of Orléans and crown the king. That's simple enough, isn't it?'

I laughed to hide my anxiety. Simple words, yes, but great and difficult plans.

'Nothing is greater than God,' Jehanne said, sensing my discomfort, 'nothing will defeat Him or His messenger.'

The next day, while Jehanne met the dauphin's councillors, I explored Chinon. It was a pleasant market town, bustling with life. No one here seemed to be in any hurry to discuss the war. In fact it seemed so far away that it might be a story, a traveller's tale told by a winter fire. The scenes I had witnessed on the frontiers of Reims had long faded from the forefront of my mind, though as I discovered in dreams for years afterwards, such things leave their scar.

When Jehanne returned, we met again in her room. There was no news. The councillors were divided, but on the whole she seemed more optimistic about meeting the dauphin and hoped to be summoned into his presence the next day.

'Are you content, Mariane?' Jehanne said.

I nodded but, with a serious expression, I reached for my slate, turned it over and made a rough drawing of a hen.

Jehanne laughed out loud and said, 'Polly! She's with Uncle Durand!' and I tapped my chest with my fist to show my relief.

Jehanne enclosed my two hands in hers. 'I know what's to come. I have seen myself riding at the head of the troops, I'm carrying a banner—I have the design—' She released my hands and sat back. 'You must help me make it. Lend me your slate—'

While Jehanne sketched the design for her banner, I sat wide-eyed, taking stock. This was the old Jehanne, but also the new, someone taller, stronger, more determined than ever, her face glowing at the sound of her own words. As she went on with this mission, she seemed more and more like a puny David facing all-powerful Goliath, or like a candle flame in a raging storm, and I feared for her.

She was finishing the sketch when de Poulengy walked in with a bundle of men's clothes. He dumped them in front of me.

'For you, Mariane.'

I faltered, aghast. For me? Then I shook my head vigorously, but de Poulengy nodded and with an amused grin on his face laid out the garments one by one on the bed. He laughed out loud when I growled at him. I looked down at the man's grey doublet, the tunic, the hose, then snatched them up and held them tight in my fist.

As the door closed on de Poulengy, I swung round on Jehanne, and shook the clothes at her, then threw them to the ground.

'Don't look at me like that, Mariane,' she said and shrugged. 'It had to be. It's logical, you see? Who would listen to me in my peasant girl clothes? Remember what happened in Vaucouleurs? Time's running out. Who would follow me into battle if I dressed like a woman who herds cows and pulls turnips?' She leaned forward to press home her argument. 'The men have to believe I can lead them. God has given me direction on this. Whether I will it or not, I must play the part of a soldier, Mariane. I have to take the lead, I have to stand at the head of the French army confronting the English. Me. It's a terrible thought, isn't it? My heart fails me to think about it.' She ran her hand over her cropped hair. 'I had thought I might escape it and simply sit in a strongroom, like the dauphin's keep there—' She gestured through the window to the castle visible on the skyline. 'High and far above the battlefield itself. I would issue daily orders, direct from God, and leave the rest to the seasoned warriors. But it's not to be.' She picked up the clothes.

'Come on. It's practical,' she shrugged.

No. For a woman to dress as a man still seemed against nature. I shook my head.

'Mariane, are you with me?' she said.

Yes, yes. How can you doubt it? Tears sprang into my eyes as I bowed my head to her.

'Well, then,' she said and held out the clothes. And so, with great misgiving, God forgive me, I put them on.

When I was ready, tugging at the tunic where it barely covered my modesty, I stood for Jehanne's inspection.

'Is this what I look like?' Jehanne said. I nodded and we giggled nervously and clutched each other's elbows, then stood back, studying each other, standing with our feet apart like young men.

For a single breath, we stared at each other. Then, like an extinguished flame, the joy left us. Jehanne's eyes filled with tears, her chin trembled, and the corners of her mouth turned down. Silent tears began to course down her cheeks and she covered her face with her hands.

'What have I done?' she whispered. 'God help me—what have I done?'

All I could do was put my arms around her and hold tight until her sobbing was over. But we kept our men's clothes.

That night her prayers were long and hard. We prayed together, but not from the missal. Jehanne's prayers were all cries to God to release her from her mission, to take away the burden from her shoulders, so that she could go home; to send someone else into battle against the English, a seasoned warrior, better suited. Then as time passed, the prayers changed to desperate repetitions of the Ave Maria and the Credo. After that, there was a long pause when Jehanne simply rocked backwards and forwards, backwards and forwards, clenching her hands in her lap, the knuckles white with strain. Finally she stopped and breathed more easily and rested, for so long that I thought she might be falling asleep. Just when I was on the point of moving myself to try to make some sort of pillow to put under her head, she spoke again. 'Thy will be done. Thy will be done. Not mine, Father, but Thy will be done.' And then, after a further pause of a few minutes, came the whispered, 'Amen.'

In silence we got ready for bed. When I was sure Jehanne was soundly asleep, I crept to the night stand. There I took up a bowl, placed it on top of my head, then picked up the shears and cut off all the hair I could reach, below the rim, well above my ears. Then I put down the bowl, gathered the hair and threw it into the fire, making a wish as

I did so that God would keep me safe on this dangerous quest. The hair, part of me, my pride, my vanity, crackled and sizzled as it burnt, making a fine blaze and stink, but my heart turned to stone as I watched. It was as if I were burning the old Mariane and taking on a new character, not a powerless girl any more, but someone who could look and act like a soldier, at Jehanne's side, come what may.

I poured water into a wide shallow bowl and when the surface was quite still I looked down into it and studied my new reflection. There I was, Mariane Eloise de Courcey, daughter of François de Louviers. Supporter of the Maid. Soldier of France. There could be no turning back.

CHAPTER ELEVEN
THE DAUPHIN

The next day, we woke early and went straight away to hear Mass and, for the first time in my life, it was not a duty or a thankless chore, but a great comfort to me.

There was no news from the dauphin: another day lost, but we kept ourselves busy. After breakfast, Jehanne asked me to write to her mother, giving news of her progress. As I was setting a wax seal on the letter, a horseman clattered into the inn yard. Within minutes someone came running upstairs with loud, clomping steps. The door burst open.

'*Pierre!*' Jehanne's brother caught her up and whirled her around.

'Look at you!' he said. 'Bless me—must I call you Jehan, like a boy, from now on?'

We ordered more wine, bread, and cheese, and I settled myself to hear all Pierre's news.

'I was writing to maman, just this minute,' Jehanne said. 'How is she?'

'She's well and preparing to go to Puy.'

'To the shrine?'

'Yes. She's going to pray for you and the success of your mission. But she wants news that you are safe in Chinon, before she leaves.'

'And here it is!' Jehanne said, brandishing the letter.

'And my father?' she said, waiting, alert, for Pierre's answer.

'Oh, you know.'

'Was he very angry?'

'For a day and a night. He went missing—to this day I don't know where he went, no one does, not even maman—but then he came back and got on as if nothing had changed. He's kept up the story that you are in Burey, helping Uncle Durand. But the rumours are spreading, Jehanne. The day's quickly coming when he'll have to face up to the fact that his daughter is the Maid of Lorraine and no longer little Jehanne.' Pierre hugged his sister. 'It's so good to be here.' He let her go, then added, 'Some folk have privately told me that they know the truth—how, I've no idea—but they say they've always known you were different, called by God, and they've tied prayer rags to the Fairy Tree, to ask God to grant you success and a safe return.'

I smiled at the mention of the tree. It was an ancient weeping beech in Domrémy, with a vast leafy canopy, like a domed roof, where we used to meet to sing and dance and make wishes.

Pierre sat at the table and said, 'Now I'm here and ready for action. What's the news?'

As Pierre ate his way through a hunk of cheese and a wedge of flat bread, Jehanne told him about the delay in seeing the dauphin.

'And what do you want me to do? What's my task?'

'I need you to help with battle practice for anyone willing to attend. All those who want to fight, especially beginners.

Everyone can do something to defend themselves. We've had to set up outside the town gates, so that we don't alarm the dauphin. You'll have to send out word, discreetly mind, that we're looking for anyone willing to bear arms.'

And that is what Pierre did. Over the coming weeks, both Jehanne and I honed our skills with lance and sword at his camp, though Jehanne said she hoped she would never have to use them in battle. 'God defend me from killing anyone,' she said, and I comforted her, saying that it probably wouldn't come to that. But, of course, I was wrong.

Finally the message came that Jehanne was to attend the dauphin and, after breakfast, a small troop of us set off up the main street of Chinon towards the royal stronghold, on the rise overlooking the town.

As we walked over the drawbridge and entered the gatehouse, I looked round in awe. The place was impregnable. Massive stone walls without windows reared up on every side into the sky. High battlements topped the towers, each marked by archery slits. The gatehouse entrance was a dark tunnel, the only light striking from murderholes overhead, through which hidden archers watched our progress. At the slightest hint of a threat, they would rain down a storm of deadly arrows. My neck twitched and my head shrank into my shoulders until we were out of that hideous tunnel.

In the inner courtyard, there was an official escort waiting to take Jehanne to the dauphin. Her own supporters, de Poulengy and de Metz, fell back courteously as the master of the dauphin's household, Louis de Bourbon, came forward to accompany her. The yard was crowded with silent onlookers, grooms and kitchen maids, ostlers and smiths. I followed Jehanne nervously, watched by so many eyes.

My heart faltered again as we entered the grand hall. It was full to overflowing with the dauphin's own courtiers. Over three hundred men, as I discovered later, the flower of French nobility, dressed in their fine coats of dazzling colours and rich fabrics, stood to watch our approach.

They were all seasoned warriors, experienced in the war against the English, rich landowners with crowds of retainers to do their every bidding, men who must bow down to Jehanne and follow her if her mission was to go on. It seemed an impossible task.

But the court of the dauphin awaited us, prepared to listen. De Baudricourt's letter had done that much.

As we came to a halt in the space in the middle of the room, Jehanne seized the initiative.

'Where's the dauphin?' she said, brushing aside all ceremony. There were audible gasps. 'I must see him.'

In the midst of all this splendour she made a striking sight: like a sober young prince, all in black.

Still silent, Louis de Bourbon held up his hand, then, when everyone was settled again, he spoke to her.

'You are Jehanne d'Arc?' he said.

'Of course I am,' Jehanne replied, impatiently.

'You will get no further hearing if you disregard the respect owed to the throne and its representatives,' said de Bourbon, firmly.

'I'm sorry, my lord,' said Jehanne and she removed her hat and swept into a long low bow which she gave to the whole room. 'Thank you for admitting me to this gathering. I apologize if I seem rude. My manners are lacking, since France hangs by a thread. My mission is urgent, my lord. Time is short and I must see the dauphin.'

'And so you shall. I am he.' A man in red broke free of the crowd and came to stand before her.

'You are not, my lord. Forgive me, but you are not.'

'No, quite right, maid: it is I,' said another, in gold and purple this time.

'No. No. Please don't insult me, lords, with your games.' Jehanne pushed her way through the crowd, then went to kneel in front of a slight young man, thin, with a careful gaze.

'Liege,' she said and bowed her head. The dark cloak he was wearing swung aside to reveal blue velvet robes, embroidered with the royal emblem, the pale gold fleur de lys. Jehanne couldn't disguise her relief. 'Liege,' she repeated.

'What is it, maid?' said the man.

Jehanne looked up at him. 'Most noble lord dauphin, I am come, and am sent by God, to bring help to you and your kingdom.'

There was a long pause, then as the Dauphin moved away to study the rest of us, leaving Jehanne still on her knees, the court broke into applause. Had Jehanne passed a test? It seemed so. The courtiers were impressed that she was able to pick out the dauphin, but I thought anyone with intelligence would not have been fooled by the charade, and I hoped that the dauphin had not devised the trick himself.

As he passed, the courtiers fell elegantly, one by one,

into deep bows and courtesies, including, as he approached, Pierre, de Poulengy, de Metz. I was next and, forgetting myself, I started a courtsey, which I quickly changed into a bow. The dauphin's lips twitched into a smile.

From under my brows, I studied him. So this was the dauphin, Charles, who would be King Charles VII when he was finally crowned in the cathedral at Reims. I blinked. My heart thudded. Majesty. I was in the presence of God's servant, the future king, divinely appointed to rule. In supreme power over us all.

From the corner of my eye I watched him go back to Jehanne, then reach to touch her shoulders as if knighting her after a battle. He raised her up until they stood face to face.

'We have a great deal to discuss,' he said, leading her away through a door into a private room to the right of the fireplace. He refused to let anyone else into the room and once the door closed on them, a guard snapped to attention in front of it, his lance ready across his chest.

Jehanne and the dauphin stayed in there long after the rest of us were dismissed. By the end of the day, she had won his support. After this, for the first part of her mission, there were few who stood in her way.

CHAPTER TWELVE
THE MYSTERIOUS STRANGER

The dauphin gave Jehanne his support, but it took weeks to persuade him to take action, while the English conquerors continued their advance.

Of the seven deadly sins, sloth—accidie—is perhaps the worst. Grandmère taught me to watch for it: indecision, inertia, call it what you will, the refusal to act.

The dauphin was scared, caught in its toils, I could tell. He was a man in retreat. Chinon was hundreds of miles from where he should have been: in Reims, where he was to be crowned king, or in Paris, the capital and centre of power. No wonder the people had lost heart, no wonder the English were winning.

Jehanne's task was great, and I wondered how she would persuade the dauphin to set out on his journey to Reims. If we French were ever to unite and fight for our country, he must step forward as king and claim his throne.

But Charles was not a natural leader. He was thin-limbed, undernourished and, worse, there was a hopeless look in his eyes, like that of a child used to being beaten who cannot predict when the rod will appear. I saw him flinch at the bark of a dog and shiver at the slam of a door. Such a man doesn't need enemies: he defeats himself.

Jehanne and I made use of these long, stale hours. We practised our battle skills under Pierre's skilled tutelage, and encouraged those men and women who had joined us to do the same. Jehanne was becoming skilled with the quarterstaff, learning moves that she also used with the sword—thrust, tail-thrust, block, side-stroke, and side-sweep—though, as she said often enough, she hoped that she wouldn't have to fight, because she certainly couldn't kill anybody. Nevertheless, she practised hard, just in case, saying she wouldn't ask the soldiers to do something she wasn't prepared to do herself.

I could still beat her in a bout, but she had a quick eye and a strong arm, and she quickly learned to sit safely in the high war saddle, gripping her charger with her knees so that her arms were free to wield her lance and sword. She forged a strong bond with her horse, feeding him herself and grooming him after every exercise, and he responded, watching for her every morning with his nose over the stable door and noisily whickering as soon as she came into view.

One morning, during the second month of our stay, I think, we were together in the stable yard, dressing the horses, when a stranger on horseback arrived. I tapped Jehanne's arm urgently to point him out. The man seemed very mysterious, closely wrapped in a long black cloak. His black horse had no identifying harness.

'I've no idea who he is,' she whispered, shaking her head as, with a practised hand, the man threw the reins over his horse's head and dismounted. A silver hauberk and greaves glinted between the folds of his cloak. I tugged Jehanne's sleeve.

'Mm—expensive. Someone important,' she said. Over the back of my horse, I squinted at him again. He had no weapons, helmet, or shield. Not come from battle then. Jehanne went back to brushing her horse's mane, but something about the man intrigued me and I kept an eye on him.

Horse and rider seemed exhausted. The horse's gleaming flanks were crisped with mud, its shoulders steamed from exertion, and its teeth sneered from between drawn-back lips as it gasped for air. The rider's cloak clung to him, heavy with wet, and irritably he pushed it off his shoulder to reach for a wallet strapped to his saddle. His face was grim and well-bearded, as though he had ridden for days without rest.

As a castle groom appeared to lead his horse into a stable, he cast a glance at Jehanne and me, and seemed about to speak. I looked at Jehanne, but she hadn't noticed and went on brushing her horse, and the man seemed to think better of it.

Before setting off for the castle, he looked back again, as if he were studying Jehanne for some reason, but again he turned away.

My heart stopped. As his cloak swung aside, I saw the device on his tunic. It was two blue arrowheads on a white circle, the chevrons placed on the roundel, as they were on the badge that my father had left. Now my heart knocked like a hammer. Was this man from my father's household? He seemed too high ranking to be a servant. Was he a member of my father's family? One of my own relatives?

'Holà! Jehanne!' It was Pierre.

'Holà, frère de ma vie!' Jehanne kissed her brother on both cheeks. 'How many turned up this morning?'

'Another three dozen, I think—Mariane!' said Pierre, smiling, and I acknowledged his greeting then got on with my task, as he and Jehanne discussed details of the training schedule and the numbers of folk turning up every day, wanting to fight for France.

My heart still pounded with the thought that maybe the stranger was my relative. Perhaps I had half-sisters and brothers, aunts and uncles, grandparents, a whole family of my own, on my father's side. I had to know.

I watched the stranger walk into the gatehouse and, gesturing an excuse to Jehanne, quickly followed.

As I ran into the inner courtyard, I saw him on the far side, deep in conversation with Louis de Bourbon. Both glanced at me, but seeing, as they thought, only a stable lad, continued their talk. I walked slowly towards them, then went past into the main keep, as if I were on an errand, but secretly darted back and slipped into the shadows, where I could hear what they said.

De Bourbon asked about the state of the road to Reims.

'It will be impassable soon, after all this rain,' said the stranger. 'It's already clogged with mud and flooded in places. The river's too deep for a traveller on foot, but horses will carry you through, if you don't delay.'

'I'll inform the dauphin. And you must rest and take food. Henri—' De Bourbon summoned a page, and I pressed myself deep into my hiding-place as the men moved past, then, walking silently behind them at a safe distance, I followed.

'I hope you're well-provisioned. There are peasants coming here, hordes of them, hundreds. They're deserting the villages, heading this way. Something's stirred them up. It's not the enemy; the situation hasn't changed as far as the English are concerned. No, this is something else. They've abandoned their homes, they've not even poisoned the wells, they're on the move and they're coming here. They're starving. Things could turn nasty.'

'Starving or not, we can't feed them,' said de Bourbon. They stopped and I ducked behind a pillar.

'They seek a Saviour. They say the Saviour of France is here. A ridiculous tale, *n'est-ce pas*? But they believe it, you see. Faith moves mountains.' He made to walk on, but de Bourbon held him back.

'Whom do they mean? The dauphin?'

'No. I had the same thought, but no.'

'Look, you'd better tell me exactly what you've heard.'

'Apparently it's some girl. They call her the Maid.' He laughed and paused, but de Bourbon stayed silent.

'I must say they're very specific. Her name is Jehanne D'Arc, she was born in Lorraine, at Domrémy, and they believe that God and his saints give her messages.' Again he paused and again de Bourbon was silent.

'They say, milord, that she will deliver Orléans, then take the dauphin to Reims to be crowned king.'

I glimpsed the stranger's face and saw his casual smile fade, as he took in de Bourbon's expression. Then he gave a loud, mocking laugh.

'Forgive me, milord, I see I bring stale news. *Dieu*, but I never thought to see a prince of the blood taken in by this fantasy.'

De Bourbon signalled the page forward again, and said, 'It's true, the Maid is here. I ask you to reserve your judgement, milord, until you meet her.'

No more was said and they disappeared inside the castle. So, I was no wiser as to the stranger's name, but it seemed from de Bourbon's courteous welcome that he was nobly born.

Jehanne was out on the lists when I arrived back at the stables, but the rest of the stranger's party had arrived, along with his equipment and baggage, and his squire was brushing his master's horse. I sat down to watch and, after a few minutes, as I knew he would, the boy broke the silence.

'You'd think as 'e'd take better care. Look at this.' He lifted the horse's right back leg to show me that the shoe was missing.

'He should 'ave 'ad him shod straightaway. 'E's ridden him I don't know 'ow many miles in this state. It's a wonder the horse isn't lame.'

I dug into the breast of my tunic to find my slate and chalk.

What's his name? I wrote, then twisted the slate round for the groom to read.

He glanced at the slate. ''S no use showin' me that. I can't read,' he said. I was about to rub the slate clean when de Bourbon appeared. Automatically he took the slate and read it aloud. 'What's his name?' Then he smiled at me and looked questioningly at the groom. 'Warrior,' he said. 'His name's Warrior.' De Bourbon grinned at me, then patted the horse and passed on.

When he was out of sight I grabbed the groom's sleeve, pointed to the slate and the horse and shook my head vigorously.

'Not the 'orse's name? What you on about?'

'Ma . . . ma . . .' I growled, signing a beard with a sharp pincer movement of thumb and fingers round my chin.

'Man?' said the groom and I nodded and grinned. I could have kissed him. 'My master? His name?'

Yes. I nodded again.

'De Louvier. Gaston de Louvier,' he said, and got on with oiling the horse's sore legs.

Flushed with pleasure, I turned away and grinned again. De Louvier. My father's name. This stranger might be my father's brother. De Louvier. That would have been my name, if my parents had married. I reached into my pocket and closed my fingers on my father's badge.

This man was my relative. I had a family on my father's side.

CHAPTER THIRTEEN
REVELATION

There were so many danger signs but, dazzled by joy, I ignored them. All I could see was that here was a link with my father's family, Sir Gaston de Louvier, my father's brother.

And the next day, between chores, I trailed him like a motherless puppy, watching and waiting for my chance to meet him face to face.

But fate stepped between us. Each time I saw him alone, someone else accosted him first, so I was prevented from showing him my badge and revealing my identity.

The day after that he spent closeted with the dauphin, so I stayed in the stable, from where I could keep a weather eye on the door of the royal apartment.

I spent the time grooming Castanier, though he didn't really need it. All morning, the door opened only twice: once for a page to go in and out, and once for de Bourbon, but there was no sign of Sir Gaston.

In the stall next to mine, Sir Gaston's squire was cleaning his master's gear: he had finished the harness and bridle and now, having made himself a comfortable place to sit by throwing a blanket over a hay bale, he sat polishing the saddle, feeding the fine leather with scented oil. While he polished the leather in a slow rhythm, he kept glancing up at me. When I refused to meet his eye he began to talk anyway. Few can stand silence for long.

'The name's Didier,' he called. 'I'm squire to Sir Gaston, or I soon will be, when I've served me time. 'Spect you've 'eard of Sir Gaston. The dauphin's right 'and, they call 'im; the royal spymaster. Ever so 'igh up, 'e is. In a position o' trust.' As he stopped and began to whistle through his teeth, I moved round Castanier and hung over the wooden partition between the stalls.

'Who are you, then?' he said, and when I mooed my response, he glanced up and said, 'Lost yer tongue? Somebody cut it aht, did they?' and he put the saddle aside and came towards the barrier. ''Ere,' he said, 'open yer marf, let's 'ave a look, then. Did it 'urt?'

When he got close, I growled and reached over to give him a good shove and he fell back into his seat.

'Orlright, calm down. I was on'y bein' friendly.' He set to with his task again, but didn't speak, so I leant over the barrier as far as I could and tapped Sir Gaston's shield, with its white and blue device, my father's device, and raised my eyebrows at Didier, as if to ask him about it. He took the hint.

'Famille de Louvier. Nobility from up north, near Rouen. I've never been to the estate, mind, but I've 'eard as 'ow it's massive, a fahsend acres at least. There's a big manor 'ouse, and some farms and villages, and a big church, practickly a cafedral. I'd like to see that one day, but I can't see that 'appenin'. Not in the foreseeable, like. Sir Gaston's never been there for years. 'E's been too busy prancin' about in England, gathering information for the dauphin. I was wiv 'im. o'course. Important information, vital to national security.' He paused to let me take in this impressive information, then went on, 'The estate's called La Paix. 'E could do wiv goin' there, you know. It's on 'is mind, I know it is. There's fings to sort out.' He stared into space and his eyes glazed over.

What things? Anxious to keep him talking, I banged the top of the stall with the flat of my hands and he looked at me in surprise, but then he leaned forward over the saddle and fixed my eyes with his. 'If I tell yer, yer won't say anyfink, will yer? On'y 'e might send me packing with sumfink to show for it, if 'e catches me talking about 'is private business.' He paused then went on, 'Well, Sir Gaston was the younger bruvver, see. François, the elder, the rightful heir, 'e copped it at Agincourt, and, because Sir Gaston was a prisoner in England at the time, the estate passed into the safekeeping of 'is sister. Now Sir Gaston's back and 'e wants to claim the estate. But 'is sister, what was looking after things—she passed the whole lot, the running of it, that is, to the church, 'cause she's turned 'erself into a healer—well, she's a widderwoman now, so what else can she do?

'Well, Sir Gaston, 'e don't like that. Especially when 'is sister is still harping on about how La Paix should go to the rightful heir, what her brother François chose. But Sir Gaston's determined to get La Paix back into 'is own 'ands. Well, 'e should, shouldn't 'e? It's 'is family land, innit? It belongs to the de Louviers.'

He sighed, spat on the saddle and rubbed it, then lifted it off his lap, stood up and came closer. 'I fink 'e's got it marked dahn, for when 'e retires from 'is himportant jobs. I bet 'e'll go straight back there, when this lot's finished.'

He jerked his head at the shield, to say, this war with the English, then went on, 'One day, 'e'll say, "Didier? Saddle the 'orse. We're goin' 'ome, to La Paix." I bet 'e will.'

As Didier turned to hang up the saddle, I frowned. La Paix. Would I ever go there? I'd like to see it. Lost in thought, I suddenly realized that Didier was speaking to me.

'You deaf as well as dumb?'

I glared at him over the barrier as he repeated his question.

'Squire to the Maid, are yer? 'Ere, is she really who she says she is? Does she work miracles? I'd like to see a miracle, like what it says in the Bible. I'd like to see 'er do a real miracle. Course there is those what says she's lyin'. Some even say,' he lowered his voice, 'that she's a *witch*! Wearing men's clothes. It's not decent.'

I barked and growled at him and, keeping my sights on him, made my way round to his side of the barrier. Didier took a stance and said, 'Come on then, come on then, dafty—' calling me out with his fists. Raising mine, I dashed at him, but he ducked and I missed. 'Come on, come on, lame-brain—' Grinning, he danced about in the open space at the head of the stalls where there was room for us to fight. 'Fight for your master-mistress!'

I had just landed a useful punch on the side of his head, when Sir Gaston's voice rang across the yard. 'Didier! A horse—now!'

We broke apart and Didier grinned at me. 'See you later!' he said, turning to lead out one of the horses.

I moved to the doorway and watched Sir Gaston mount up and gallop away. Then I ran up the steps by the gatehouse and watched from the parapet as he sped along the road to Reims, and my heart swelled with pride. When the war was over perhaps I could go with him. To my father's home, to La Paix.

CHAPTER FOURTEEN
MY FATHER'S LEGACY

My chance to reveal myself to Sir Gaston came during the feast given to welcome him back to the court. Louis de Bourbon had given me permission to serve the wine on the high table, to give me the true flavour of a royal occasion. What I really wanted was the chance to approach Sir Gaston, who would be seated there, at the dauphin's right hand. My plan was to show him the badge.

The hall glowed with the rich colours of costly velvet and silk, azure and indigo, royal purple and gold, and with the sheen of steel armour that caught the reflection of firelight, dancing yellow and orange flames from two fires, one either end of the room.

Above the long tables, set with the gold and silver dishes and trenchers that the dauphin insisted on, hung the royal standards, suspended from the rafters. Gold fleur de lys on blue silk, two or thee hundred, stretching the entire length of the hall, lazily coiling and unfolding in the eddies of warm air.

The high stone walls, the vaulted ceiling, absorbed the sound of the company: knights and squires feasting, the constant to-ing and fro-ing of servants, the crackle of the fires, the restless fluttering of the hooded falcons, and the snores of the great hunting hounds.

They ate well. The cooks brought in a succession of dishes: roast sucking pig, wild boar, venison, beef and ham, and a roast swan, wrapped in its feathers as if still alive. As I stood behind the dauphin, my flagon of wine at the ready, the swan made me think of Polly and I wondered if she was content in Burey and I wished her, with all my heart, a full dish of corn and fresh water, green leaves to peck at and a clean bed of straw.

I watched Jehanne who had insisted on sitting below the salt, with those of lower rank. A richly decorated silver salt server divided them from those who sat above the salt with the dauphin.

Jehanne ate hardly anything. She thought feasting a waste of time and money when the French people, still starving in the siege of Orléans, were waiting to be set free. But she held her peace, leaving it, as always, to God to bring the dauphin to his senses.

Frustrated in my efforts to speak to Sir Gaston, who obviously thought servants were invisible, I studied his profile as he silently ate and watched the assembled company. Did he look like my father? Did my father have that black hair? Was that my father's nose? A straight Roman nose, very proud, a little arrogant even, but that's not a bad thing in a warrior, I thought, defending them both, uncle and father, against the slur.

Suddenly I shot to attention, almost spilling my wine. The dauphin had raised his right forefinger: the signal for more to drink. With great dignity I walked forward and, as his fingers closed over the stem of his goblet, I leant between him and my uncle and carefully filled it up with claret. Then I stepped back, but not to my former position.

The two were beginning to talk and perhaps I would learn more about my uncle, so, trying to blend into the tapestry hunting scene behind me, I stayed as close as I could

At first it was just boring stuff about England where Sir Gaston had been to negotiate the release of prisoners, but I pricked up my ears when I heard him mention La Paix.

'As you know, my brother, François, was head of the family when my father died. Then when François was killed at Agincourt, I should have stepped into his place; I'm sure that's what my father intended. But I was delayed in England, and my sister took charge, and now, recently widowed, she seeks solace in religion and has passed the estate into the hands of the church. Pah!' Gaston spat his disgust on to the sanded floor.

The dauphin took a sip of his wine, then said lazily, 'Surely you have a claim?' He sounded bored, but I was fascinated.

'I can do nothing, sire. The trouble began with my brother. If only he had made a will—' He looked at the dauphin hopefully.

'My hands are tied, Gaston. I wish I could help, but I daren't risk taking sides. There are so many claims of this nature. Leave it to the lawyers. It seems unlikely that your brother did not leave a will. I remember my father talking of him with great respect. Surely Sir François would have kept his affairs in strict order.'

'There was a will, of sorts, a somewhat outlandish document. It was a travesty.'

'How so?'

'Why, in it my brother left everything to a woman, my

liege. To his mistress. I knew it had to be false. I destroyed it, of course.'

Sir Gaston reached forward and tugged at the wing of the swan. When it resisted he dug the fingers of one hand into the pure white feathers, and held the neck with the other, as if he were throttling it. With a shock, I noticed how blunt his nails were, how rough and dirty his hands.

'Let Henri carve for you,' said the dauphin.

'No, liege, there's no need,' replied Sir Gaston and, with a great effort, he tore the wing from the breast, twisting it until the joint broke apart, then, holding the wing like a fan in front of his mouth, sank his teeth into the shoulder meat.

'Who was François's mistress?' asked the king.

'Her name was Eloise de Courcey.'

His bitter tone froze my blood. Sir Gaston was talking about my mother.

'De Courcey,' repeated the dauphin. 'I'm afraid I don't know the name. Nobly born? Surely?'

'No, no, liege. Eloise de Courcey was nobody. She was a farm girl. It was a grand passion, soon expired. The girl, pregnant, left and went back to her mother in Reims when he went to Agincourt.'

'Where is this Eloise now? Still in Reims?'

'She's dead, liege. Killed in an English raid, about a year ago.'

'And the child? It lived?'

'Oh yes, sire. The child, a girl, was brought up by her mother in Reims. When her mother was killed, the girl escaped.'

Escaped? It was a strange word to use.

'Forget her, Gaston. Why trouble yourself? Your brother was obviously of unsound mind when he dispensed La Paix in such a bizarre fashion, and if you've already destroyed the will—'

'I have tried to claim the estate, my liege, but there is the matter of my brother's seal, the de Louvier seal. My sister thinks he sent it to the de Courcey woman, and without it my claim is weak. The Church keeps a tight grip on La Paix, in stewardship for whoever possesses the seal. This child, if she has it, could claim the estate. I must find her. If she has the seal, a fistful of gold will surely wrest it from her.'

'Do you have lawyers?'

'Yes, liege. Guilbert de Poitiers, Guy de Conte.'

'Men of fine reputation.'

'Maybe so, but the law says that only the seal will secure my claim to La Paix. I have to find it. It's a tiresome difficulty but not insurmountable. The girl's the only clue to its whereabouts.'

'And what have you done about finding her?'

'I started with the priest in Reims. He was easily bought. These churchmen are not heroes, sire. The girl had a small legacy from François—missal and so on—the priest searched for the seal, but found nothing.'

'Perhaps he took it.'

'No, liege. Unfortunately, Cornelius turned traitor—he bolted for England, the fool. He carried some gold and items of some value, loot from the village. He was thoroughly searched and questioned,' Gaston smirked unpleasantly, 'and gave us everything, including his life. I'm certain he did not have the seal.'

'Hm.' The dauphin sipped his wine, then murmured, 'Well done, Gaston. We're well rid of turncoats.'

Sir Gaston leaned back in his chair. 'I must find the girl. There was a rumour that she left Lorraine with this Maid they speak of. The Maid is here, isn't she?'

'She is. In this very room. Let's ask her.'

Just as the dauphin raised his left forefinger to summon his page, the doors burst open and de Bourbon strode in, pushing his way past the armed guards who had automatically crossed their lances.

The dauphin stood up. 'What is it?'

'There are hundreds of people at the gates, my liege. They are starving and calling for the Maid.'

Jehanne got to her feet. 'In God's name we must feed them,' she called over the heads of the knights at the table.

'Of course,' the dauphin replied. 'De Bourbon, see to it.'

Sneaking away from the high table, I hurried out of the hall in the wake of Jehanne, de Bourbon, and several servants who peeled off to gather stores from the buttery. Others wheeled handcarts into the courtyard and collected rope and cloths to parcel up the provisions into suitable rations.

I found Jehanne deep in conversation with de Bourbon.

'Mariane,' she said, happy to see me. 'We're going to be very busy for the next few hours.' I plucked her tunic, desperate for her to come with me to a quiet place to share my thoughts. But all she said was, 'Come and help. There's a lot to do. Could you divide up the cheese?'

Reluctant, I followed her, my head buzzing as I searched for some answers. There was something wrong with Sir

Gaston's account of my mother's death. *Killed in an English raid?* How did he know? Warned by a sixth sense I glanced up to see him behind me, heading for the stables with a companion. '. . . *the girl escaped*.' The cold, hard tone of his voice rang in my mind like a death knell.

Horses were brought out for the two men. As his companion mounted, Sir Gaston walked round his horse, examining the hooves. I reached down for some mud and smeared it over my cheeks, in case he noticed me. He couldn't possibly have known who I was and, anyway, I was wearing boy's clothes, but having heard his talk at dinner, I was terrified.

'Wait, Ralph. I see it,' he called to his companion. He unsheathed a dagger from his belt and used it to pick out a stone from one of the back hooves. Trembling, I shrank into the shadows.

I recognized his dagger, with its distinctive line of rubies, like drops of blood, from hilt to point. When Jehanne and I were attacked in the wood outside Domrémy, he was there! He was the leader of the gang who had attacked us. He was in league with the English. With wide eyes, I watched him mount up.

'Keep a look out for the girl,' Sir Gaston said. 'Discreetly. No need for others to know my business.'

'If she is here, I'll find her.'

The truth hit me like a blow. I had been his target, not Jehanne. As the other man gathered his reins, he swore and pulled off his glove.

'What is it?'

'Hornet stings!' the man called. 'I ran into a swarm of them this morning. *Diable*! They itch like the devil.'

Sir Gaston shouted over his shoulder: 'You need garlic. It's a sovereign remedy.'

'Turned healer, Gaston?' shouted the man, rubbing his hand on his saddle.

'No, it's something I learned in Reims, when I visited the de Courcey woman.'

'I hear you gave her a worse sting than a hornet's, that day.'

'I did indeed!' Sir Gaston laughed. They pricked spurs, then galloped off in a cloud of dust.

The gate slowly closed. I stood there, as if carved from stone. This man, my father's brother, Sir Gaston de Louvier, had been there when my mother was murdered. '*Crushed garlic . . . My mother's been stung by a hornet. This eases the pain.*'

While I was running into the wood, while I was escaping, Sir Gaston had murdered my mother.

CHAPTER FIFTEEN
PREPARATIONS FOR WAR

In the days that followed I was plunged into a wilderness of spirit. Without warning, the world had changed. It was cold and all-powerful, and there was no help anywhere.

With eyes of stone, and a will of iron, I watched de Louvier, my heart set on revenge.

De Louvier soon discovered from Jehanne that I was his brother's child, but I stayed hidden. My mother's killer might kill me too once he realized that I did not have the seal. With frantic messages coming daily from Orléans, Jehanne was busy with battle preparations and had asked me to help with medicines, so I went out into the countryside, gathering my plant material, while the dauphin kept de Louvier busy at court.

Orléans. The dauphin had finally agreed to send Jehanne to lift the siege. The English were entrenched around the city in forts or 'bastilles', which they had built around churches or other abandoned buildings. There were twelve strung out round Orléans, watching all roads. The English headquarters was at St Laurent, on the north bank of the Loire. Four more forts stretched out north from St Laurent, stopping all traffic from the west. Two western 'bastilles' held the river, one on an island, the other on the south bank, at St Prive.

St Laurent had to be our main target. After that we would attack each fort in turn.

Two forts guarded the south road, a bridge over the Loire: the Bastille des Augustins and Les Tourelles, the fort of two towers. It had been built by the Orléannais to protect the city. Now it was held by the enemy.

North, west, and south of Orléans, the English sat in their forts and stopped the supply of food into the city. But to the east was a weakness: the fort of St Loup was isolated from the others. Three miles of open countryside lay between St Loup and its nearest neighbour. Three miles, unguarded.

Down eastern roads, supplies trickled into Orléans with a continuous trail of farmers' carts, mill wagons, goose girls, and cowherds. The English took no action to prevent this traffic. Perhaps they knew that these meagre provisions were not enough.

Hungry people are weak. The Orléannais would fall to their knees, then surrender for a piece of bread. The English captains had only to wait. Siege is a cruel but effective strategy.

Jehanne's plan was to enter the city, boldly with sixty carts of weapons as well as food. She would openly provoke the English to try to stop her, saying God was with us, not with them, so how could we fail? In private, I shook my head. We would be an easy target. How could we succeed?

Our journey there would take us first to Tours, where, much to Jehanne's distaste, she had an appointment with the dauphin's armourer, and from there to Blois, to collect sheep, cattle, and wheat.

*   *   *

It was the evening before our departure. Over the dauphin's castle, the sun shone low, and the clean grey stone sparkled in its rays. The sky had deepened to the blue of the Virgin's robe, the air blew clear and free. Everyone seemed to feel the blessing of God on the expedition, everyone was roused, cheerful, and busy, criss-crossing the courtyard with light feet, and happy banter. Then Jehanne sent for me. There was someone who wished to meet me. I guessed who it was.

Henri, the dauphin's page, brought me the summons and, as I had just finished packing the last parcel of lavender and tansy, I had no excuse to give for not going to her quarters.

Jehanne stood next to de Louvier. The two of them confronted me: my guardian angel on one side, my demon on the other. Gathering my courage, I nodded a brief greeting. Jehanne's eyes twinkled as she gave me an encouraging smile.

'Mariane,' she began, 'Sir Gaston is here on a personal errand.'

I looked at my enemy who, as he moved in his black war gear, filled the room like a foul stench and blotted out the light from the window, casting me into shadow. I gave him a bold, insolent stare.

'Mariane.' Ignoring my rudeness, de Louvier came close and graciously held out his hand. Watched by Jehanne, I took it. 'My child.' He threw his arms round me and drew me into a quick embrace. My heart shrivelled. 'This is a joyous occasion.'

Smiling, he let me go, then he smiled at Jehanne. Full of smiles, yes; treacherous courtesy, I thought, but I sat facing him, in the chair Jehanne offered and, keeping my face a blank, I prepared to listen to what he had to say.

Shifting his sword out of the way, de Louvier leant towards me and tapped my knee.

'I didn't think to find you dressed as a boy.'

I was so surprised at this that when he laughed, I laughed too. Then Jehanne said, 'It's practical, sire, for when we go to war.'

'Yes, yes, of course it is. Mariane. My cousin,' he said, taking my hand and smiling like a kindly physician. 'Do you know me?'

When I didn't answer, he looked at Jehanne and she explained how God had taken my voice away at the time of my mother's death. There wasn't a flicker of guilt in his face, only concern.

'It grieves me to hear of your great distress, Mariane. Your grandmother too, I hear, is dead.'

Removing my hand from his grasp, I nodded.

'Well then, let me repeat my question. Do you know me?'

I know you are Gaston de Louvier, the royal spymaster. I know that you are my mother's murderer and for that one day I will kill you. That was what I wanted to say, but the words, crammed in my throat jostling and eager, as usual fused into silence. Then Jehanne spoke for me.

'We know that you gather information for the dauphin.'

'But that's not why I'm here. This is a momentous meeting for me personally. I have been seeking you for months: you have been hard to trace. But then I caught the rumour of your cousin Jehanne and that you were with her. And that brought me to Chinon.' He paused and looked down, as if gathering his thoughts.

'I am your uncle, Mariane, your father's brother. I'm so pleased to have found you at last. We have a great deal to discuss. Will you allow Jehanne to speak for you?'

Curtly I nodded.

Jehanne said, 'Tell us, my lord, why you come after all this time. What is it, fourteen years since Agincourt, when Mariane's father died, and no word to her or her mother since?'

'Ha! You have a fighting spirit, Jehanne! You will bring the English to their knees!'

'I hope so, milord, but that's not the question here. Why have you come here now?'

'Because when my brother died, he left everything to Mariane's mother. And after her death, to Mariane. I was in England when that happened, so I had no chance to find you and make sure that his wishes were honoured.' *How the lies dripped like honey from his silken tongue.* 'But you must know, Mariane, that your mother disliked the life at La Paix, and did not take up the inheritance. And so the estate passed into the hands of my sister for safekeeping, until you were of age. As for me, well, it is only now, in recent months, when the English grip on the country is practically unbreakable, that the dauphin has summoned me to return from my duties in England. And so I come to find you, my dear.' He leaned towards me and took my hand again and I let it lie, cold and inert, in his grasp. 'Mariane de Courcey. My brother's heir.'

He looked into my eyes. 'You have the family seal, do you not? It was sent to your mother. If we don't return to La Paix with it, then the estate will be forfeit, and the church will inherit the land and the manor house and all that adheres, and you will be the loser.

'You must let me act for you. As soon as Orléans is relieved and the dauphin crowned, as soon as the tide of the war has turned, I shall accompany you and the seal to La Paix and we shall reclaim what is rightfully yours. Or, if, like your mother, you wished to renounce the inheritance, then we should discuss that option too. I am a wealthy man. I could make you rich beyond any dreaming—and be content to do so—if you wanted to give up any claim to La Paix.'

Pleased with his performance, he sat back and my heart felt wrung. He was my uncle, my father's brother, and I longed to believe him. But the Devil is the Father of Lies. So I watched de Louvier like a hawk.

'Fetch your box, Mariane. Show your uncle the contents.'

I flashed a glance at Jehanne, but she simply nodded, her face grave, and I knew I must trust her.

I fetched the box, unlocked it, and spread the contents on the table.

'Ah, François's missal,' said Gaston, passing his blunt fingers over the worn black leather. 'I have one the same, a gift from our aunt at our baptisms.' He laid the book aside and took up the glove. 'His gauntlet. What a soldier he was, Mariane. What a warrior, expert with sword and crossbow.'

He looked in the box and turned over the scrap of brown cloth. 'And the seal?'

Hastily I pulled out the badge from my tunic.

'The de Louvier emblem. Yes, yes. But what about the seal?'

Slowly, my eyes fixed on his, I shook my head. There was a pause.

'You must have seen it? A ring, a gold ring with the family crest on the boss.'

I shook my head.

Abruptly he stood up and said, with an edge to his voice, 'We can do nothing without it.'

I shrugged, packed my things back into the box and closed the lid.

'Well, perhaps you need time to remember,' he said. He clapped his hand heavily on my shoulder. 'We must meet again.' Then, smiling with cold eyes, he wagged his finger at me. 'Yes, we must.' As an afterthought, he picked up the box and held it close to his chest. 'Would you like me to take care of this for you, Mariane? I should not like to see these precious things go missing.'

Shocked, I jumped up, but Jehanne put out her hand to calm me and said, 'It will be quite safe here. I'm sure Mariane derives much comfort from keeping it by her side.' She held out her hand for the box.

Sir Gaston hesitated, then said, 'Of course,' and handed it over.

'So,' he said, moving to the door, 'you're heading for Blois?'

'Yes,' replied Jehanne. 'But we stop at Tours first. The dauphin's armourer is there. I must wear armour, they say.'

'Indeed,' said de Louvier. 'The English are not of God's party. Their arrows will not miss the Maid.'

'Then to Blois, to gather provisions. The Orléannais will fight better on full stomachs, I think.'

At the door de Louvier turned. 'God speed, Maid.'
'And you, milord. Where are you headed?'
'Poitiers, then Orléans.'
'So, we shall meet again.'
De Louvier and I held each other's eyes.
'Count on it,' he said.

CHAPTER SIXTEEN
ORLEANS

My own concerns were soon lost in the struggle to save Orléans. It would make a fine prize for the English: if the city fell, they would control the Loire and sweep relentlessly south.

Since the English controlled the north and west, Jehanne intended to approach from the south, keeping a distance, then cross the river to the east and make camp.

The priority was the safe delivery of the food, though Jehanne longed to fight and so did the men. But she soon found that the military commander of Orléans, Dunois, had his own plans. There would be no triumphal march into Orléans. Jehanne and her men must not cross the river, but were to set up camp on the south bank of the Loire. Worse, the next day Jehanne's men would be sent back to Blois to fetch more supplies.

Jehanne's eyes glittered with rage. 'In God's name, Dunois!' she cried. 'I bring you the help of the King of Heaven! Why these delays? God's help is better than any you have provided!'

'So you say, Maid.' Dunois, weary, looked away from her, into the distance.

'I come to fight. Bring me face to face with the English!'

'In good time.' Dunois turned to look at her, kindly, I thought. 'We must get these supplies into the city,' Dunois said. 'Tonight you and I shall enter Orléans together, quietly, with discretion. Show yourself to the people. Comfort them. We'll discuss tactics tomorrow.'

On the north bank of the Loire, directly opposite the camp, was the lone English outpost, St Loup. Jehanne suggested an immediate attack. Dunois said no. Nothing must jeopardize the delivery of the food.

The supplies were to be floated down to Orléans on barges, which the English would find difficult to reach. Dunois and a small troop would mount a skirmish outside St Loup, to draw enemy attention away from the barges. Jehanne must stay with her men and wait.

It was a sensible plan: the Orléannais would fight better with full stores of food and weaponry. But Jehanne, pale and fretful, paced angrily along the river bank as Dunois's men gathered, ready to cross the Loire.

There was a further delay. The river was too low for barges and the wind was from the west, the wrong direction. And, the barges were still in the city.

Surrounded, as far as the eye could see, by milling cattle and sheep, wagons of wheat and barley, with her soldiers soon to require orders, Jehanne faced Dunois.

'In God's name, His counsel is wiser than yours! Where are your barges?'

Dunois frowned at her blazing energy and had opened his mouth to reply when the cry came that the wind had changed and the water level was rising. The news spread through the camp, the men swarmed to the river to see for themselves, then cheered as a string of barges hove into view.

Jehanne, head bowed, was on her knees giving thanks.

Those nearest to her moved back, keeping a reverent distance, then stood guard while the Maid thanked God for His help.

Dunois did not see it as God's doing. I heard him speak low to his companion. 'Why do they follow her? Even the dauphin's captains obey when she speaks. This girl thinks she will raise the siege single-handed in a day. The dauphin sends us this innocent and these men follow her. Why?'

As he led his troop into the river, I wished, as I had many times, for my voice—*Because her faith is a rock.*

Jehanne and I shaded our eyes to watch the last of the cargo being loaded. Shouts and the clash of weapons from the opposite bank signalled the start of Dunois's diversion. The barges slipped unimpeded, silently, down the river to the city. The plan seemed to be working.

I glanced sideways at Jehanne. *Her faith is a rock* but it was also a heavy burden. How worn she looked. How much older. We were a long way from Domrémy, hundreds of miles, months of journeying and, in the bent of our minds, years away. We had come from farmyard to royal court, from turnip field to battle field, through loss and death, trial and torment, to stand here.

When she caught my eye, I gave her a smile of encouragement.

'Ah, yes, of course, it's good,' she replied, but she didn't smile, just went on knocking her clenched fist against her thigh.

As we followed the barges' progress there was a sudden outbreak of angry shouts from the camp. While Dunois was busy at St Loup, Jehanne's men kicked their heels, knowing that in the morning they must return to Blois.

'Listen to them, Mariane,' she said. 'Soldiers without a fight. Some talk loudly about giving up and going home. Have you heard them?' She waved a hand at the last departing barge. 'But what can I do? Dunois's right. The food comes first.' She didn't wait for my answer, but abruptly turned and strode down to the camp, where Pierre and another man were holding back a crowd of soldiers. Two men, weapons drawn, were circling each other.

'Put up your swords!' Jehanne called. The crowd parted to let us through, but the men went on baiting each other. 'Down on your knees. Beg God's forgiveness. Can't you hear the English? They're laughing. We don't need to fight the French, they say. They are defeating themselves.' As the men hesitated and looked at her, Pierre and the other man pushed them to their knees.

'Look to your gear,' she said. 'Where are your knives? Where are your shields? Where is your mail? At all times, you must be ready. The food has gone into the city, but it's not enough to sustain us all. More must be fetched from Blois. Get up.' As the men struggled to their feet, she seemed to relent her harsh treatment and said, 'You two stay here. Tonight, when I enter Orléans, you shall ride beside me.'

As the crowd dispersed, still muttering, Jehanne swung round to me. 'This delay has sapped their will, so we must ask God to strengthen it. Send out messengers. Gather the men to the field.'

* * *

I was late for the meeting and had to push my way through hundreds of jostling troops to get to the front. I had intended to join Jehanne and stand at her side, but when I caught sight of her, on a dais talking with a priest, I stopped dead.

She had put on full armour, and her warrior's splendour took my breath away. In the fire of the late afternoon sun, she shone all silver and flame, like Saint Michael himself. Her left hand rested on the pommel of her sword. Her other held high her white standard, sewn all with gold lilies, painted with a picture of Jesus seated between two angels, His right hand raised in a blessing. The standard snapped in the breeze, as if blown by the breath of God himself.

I thrilled to the sight of her, but my throat closed and my heart ached. Jehanne was no longer a simple country girl. Our lives were separating, and I knew that one day she would leave me behind, soaring ahead to a place far out of my reach.

But, gazing up at her then, I vowed with those around me, holding our fists to our hearts, that until that day I would take her command and follow her, staying true to her mission, wherever it led.

Jehanne looked down and saw me and beckoned me forward, holding out a gauntleted hand, and I reached up and pressed it to my forehead, holding it there until I had finished the prayer in my heart. *Don't let her be killed. Don't let her be killed. Don't let her be killed.*

'Why so worried? There's nothing to fear,' she said, clear-eyed and smiling, but as she let me go, I couldn't help shivering.

The men were a noisy, milling rabble, a disparate bunch, some professional soldiers, some vagabonds. Many were the boys and young men who had come to Chinon to find the dauphin's champion who would win their country back for them. They longed to fight, to prove themselves in battle. Farmers trading their ploughs for swords.

Jehanne was not deterred. Quiet and calm, she stood, like a warrior queen, sent from God. Straight and proud she watched them, then banged her standard three times on the dais, before planting it firmly at her side, as silence finally fell over the field.

When all was still, she said, 'Within these next days, Orléans will be ours.' A great cry rose up at her words. Again she signalled for silence.

'We have to prepare. Strengthen Orléans with food and weapons. Trim our gear. Steel hearts and minds. Make ready to act out God's purpose. My brothers-in-arms, pray with me.'

The men muttered and glanced at each other and I guessed that not many were used to prayers, nor had they thought of themselves before as a band of brothers. Gradually, like wheat blown by a gentle wind, they began to fall to their knees. When they were all kneeling, with their hands clasped and heads bowed, Jehanne began to recite all those words that their mothers had taught them, which they had perhaps forgotten: *Ave Maria, ora pro nobis. Pater Noster qui in caelo est. Credo in unum deum.*

When these prayers were finished, she asked the men to stand.

'God is with us.' Her voice rang across their raised faces. *'God is with us . . . with us . . . with us,'* repeated the men and the rolling sound of their deep voices was like the growl of a mighty ocean.

'We need not fear.'

'We need not fear . . . not fear . . . fear.'

She paused then called in a loud voice, 'Though I walk through the valley of the shadow of death—'

'. . . death . . . death . . .' repeated the men.

'I shall fear no evil.'

'. . . evil . . . evil . . .'

Their voices were gradually merging, until they began to speak together, saying the phrase, then pausing as if to consider its meaning:

'For Thou art with me.'

'Thy rod and thy staff.'

'They comfort me.'

With one voice, they finished the psalm together and, hearing this, I saw, as never before, that at last these men were being moulded into one body, one army under the command of the Maid, brothers-in-arms who would die for each other, and for her, and for France. An unconquerable fighting force that would carry all before it. My heart swelled in a great burst of pride and joyful tears rolled down my cheeks.

On the final word, roared out across the company, cannon fire burst from the walls of Orléans, as if the besieged people had heard the shout and wanted to add their voice and their spirit to ours.

I recognized the signal. The barges had delivered their cargo. Dunois had successfully distracted the English. The people in the city now had food and weapons. They were ready to help raise the siege.

CHAPTER SEVENTEEN
GLASDALE

'I must send a letter to the English captains,' Jehanne said, as we sat at breakfast the next day. 'Dunois drags his heels. I must do something.'

On the evening of our arrival, Dunois had accompanied Jehanne into the city to a mighty welcome. Even now, at daybreak, a crowd stood under the window of our lodgings. Jehanne went to look down at them. 'Maid!' they shouted. '*La Pucelle! Deo gratias!* Thanks be to God.' That's what they were calling her now. *La Pucelle, Fille de Dieu.* The Maid, Daughter of God.

'De Poulengy couldn't persuade them to bed, then,' Jehanne said, smiling at them and waving. 'The siege is half lifted already if the people are with us.'

She was on fire with battle plans. 'Will you write for me, Mariane? I shall send a challenge.' I took out Parchment, quill, and ink.

Jehanne paced as she spoke, still in her mail, her face glowing. 'Begin "Jhesus Maria",' she said, twisting her ring on which these two words were inscribed. We smiled, each remembering when her parents had given her the ring, a sad-happy memory of past times on the farm. I was eased to see a glimpse of the old Jehanne. But the new one soon reasserted herself.

'King of England, and you, Duke of Bedford who call

yourself Regent of France—' Jehanne dictated her words in a ringing voice, as if the little English king and his uncle, Bedford, were standing in front of her, 'deliver to the Maid, who is here sent by God, the keys of all the good towns you have violated. Go back to your own country, by God. And if you do not do so, expect the Maid, who will come to see you shortly, to your very great injury.'

Bright-eyed, she watched as I rolled the letter up tightly. 'Is it just as I said? Did you write all exactly?' she asked.

I nodded.

'So, they will read my words. So be it.' She sealed the letter, then called for heralds to deliver it to the English headquarters at St Laurent.

As the heralds left, Dunois arrived.

'You're sending a message to the English?'

'I send them a challenge,' said Jehanne.

Dunois roared with laughter. 'Do you imagine it will make any difference? They'll treat you as they do the rest of us—with utter contempt.'

'Then I'll make them pay,' Jehanne replied confidently, but she sat down with a thump on her chair and bit her lip, avoiding his eyes.

'When do we fight?' she said abruptly.

'In good time,' Dunois replied. It seemed a favourite phrase. He took bread and cheese from the table. I took some too, but Jehanne, when I offered, shook her head.

Dunois gazed out of the window. 'We must wait until all is ready. We must build up stores of weapons: for the field and for the defence of the city. Swords, pole-axes, cannonballs, missiles, arrows—we need thousands.' He

sighed and rubbed his pate. 'And we need more food.'
Jehanne slapped both hands on the table.

'We have brought food!'

'Not enough!'

Dunois jerked his thumb at the door. 'If the English
don't heed your advice and *leave* it'll take months to shift
'em. There's not enough food to keep us going. Your men
eat too! We could all starve, then the city will fall to them
anyway. We're not ready to fight.'

'I'm ready! Those people outside are ready!'

'You've accomplished a great deal, my dear. You're very
good at rasing morale. But battle's a different matter. You're
young, inexperienced, untried. You're a girl, by God. You
have much to learn.'

Jehanne jumped up, knocking her chair to the ground.
'Hear this, Dunois! I come from God, to deliver Orléans.
I am His messenger. He will not be mocked!'

'Peace, Jehanne. Peace.' Dunois waved his hand at her,
in a calming gesture. 'God helps those who help themselves.
It would be supreme folly to mount an attack now. This
battle will not be won in a day, my dear, visions or not.'

'No. In five days.' Jehanne's voice was icy. 'In five days
from now, the English will leave Orléans.'

'You're very precise.'

'My voices have said so.'

'I pray they're right,' Dunois said, tearing off another
large piece of bread.

'My troops need to fight, not go on this mission to fetch
supplies.'

'They must return to Blois for more food. Those are my
orders.'

'My orders are from God. I am to lead my men into battle and deliver Orléans.'

'*I* command here.' Dunois's voice was a blade. 'You are not a soldier. You can't command. Your role is a figure-head, a mascot, a symbol of God's blessing on our enterprise. But you won't be leading men to attack the English—'

'Listen to me, Dunois!' Jehanne planted herself in front of him and pulled down the neck of her mail shirt. 'Here is where I shall be injured in battle—' She stabbed her forefinger into her left shoulder. '—shot with an English bolt, within the next few days. I shall lead our soldiers to fight the English and I shall be wounded, but not killed. God has shown me.'

Jehanne let go of her shirt and it sprang back into place.

'My men will follow me,' she said. 'No one will stop them, neither you, nor any earthly command. The English may mock my challenge, but when I am finished with them, they will mock no more.'

She swept up her helmet and left the room.

By midday we had ridden through every part of the city and everywhere people poured into the street to see her. Their will to fight swelled like a gathering storm and took me with it. If we gave every man, woman, and child a sword or quarterstaff, could we not simply rush at the English and drive them before us? Dunois's words pulled me back. '*We must wait . . . supreme folly . . . you are not a soldier.*' I wish he had been there to see the Orléannais follow Jehanne.

'The city is like dry tinder waiting for a spark,' Jehanne

said. 'Dunois says we must wait; I'm not sure the people will wait. Dunois thinks he can order the hour of the attack, but look at them, Mariane. They know God is with them. These people will decide when to attack the English, and we must be ready.'

When we returned to our lodging, de Poulengy was waiting for us outside in the stableyard. He had grim news. Talbot had not replied to Jehanne's challenge, but was holding one of the heralds prisoner.

'Devil take him!' said Jehanne. 'God will strike him for it!' She turned her horse back into the street. 'I shall go to this Talbot and deliver my curses in person!'

De Poulengy sprang into her path and took hold of the reins. 'No! Let Dunois deal with him. There's a due process. Your herald will be safe—we will get him back—you mustn't risk yourself.'

Jehanne angrily snatched the reins from his fist, rode a little way, then turned her horse back to us. 'If they hurt him, I'll tear their heads off—'

'Don't go to Talbot, please, not the bastille at St Laurent. He would pick you off with a single shot before you got within shouting distance.'

'Glasdale, then, at Les Tourelles.'

'All right. Les Tourelles. There's a bit of a wall there for you to stand behind if they start firing.'

'De Poulengy—I'll be safe. I will! Mariane'll come with me and guard my flank.' Smiling, she looked at me and waited for an answer. I gave her a quick nod. What else could I do? My mouth was dry and my heart thumping.

'De Poulengy. Show her the surprise.' Jehanne spurred her horse and rode away.

Poulengy disappeared into one of the stables, then re-appeared leading a fine warhorse, with gold coat, white mane and tail.

'His name's Coeur-de-lion,' he said. I dismounted and, passing Castanier's reins to him, took Lionheart's. A brave name, I thought, placing my hand on the horse's smooth golden shoulder.

De Poulengy led Castanier into the stable then returned with a pack of armour.

'Sword, breastplate, and greaves.' De Poulengy laid out each item on a bench against the wall of the stable. 'Never worn armour before? I'll help you get into them.'

I pressed my head against Lionheart's white mane. He stamped his hooves, then held his head proudly while I stroked his nose and exchanged breath with him. Castanier looked out at us over the stable door and whinnied, as if she knew that her part was over. Jehanne had sent me my own destrier, a warhorse to carry me into battle. Castanier would wait here, safe, then afterwards, when it was all over, she would carry me home. I breathed in deeply. Home. Where was such a place?

'I'll come back later, after your sleep. Help you get into your gear.'

I nodded, secured Lionheart's reins to a hook in a shady place, then went inside.

The afternoon was warm and still. Most of the crowd had now left, perhaps following Jehanne. A beggarman lay snoring fitfully next to the front entrance. Two women sat opposite, backs to a house wall, their feet touching the runnel of dirty water that ran down the middle of the street. One held a silent baby to her breast. Flies droned and I put a cloth damped with woundwort over my brow, to stop them biting while I slept. But I didn't sleep.

I shall be injured in battle . . . I shall be wounded, but not killed. Jehanne had no doubt that it would happen. *'Within the next few days.'* I knew from the certainty of her tone that it was a prophecy from her voices.

Though it was warm, I pulled my blanket tightly around me. *'I shall be injured in battle.'* Battle. If this prediction came true I would be there. It would be real. There would be violence and bloodshed. I might have to kill someone. Could I do it?

'Hauberk.' De Poulengy passed me the shirt made of chain mail. I struggled a little with its weight, cursing it at first, but once I had it over my head and resting on my shoulders, it was lighter to wear than I expected and moulded easily to my shape. A church bell rang the hour—three o'clock—and we both glanced at the window. I must hurry or I would be late for my appointment at Les Tourelles.

It was a fort of two towers, built by the Orléannais, on the bridge that led south over the river Loire. It stood on the last arch before the south bank, to which it was joined by a drawbridge. When the English captured the fort, the Orléannais had broken down the arch next to it, on the side nearest the city, so that the fort lay marooned in the river, as if on an island.

'Greaves.' I stuck out each leg in turn for de Poulengy to strap on the shin guards.

'Surcoat.' The white linen surcoat with its cross of Lorraine. I put it on and shivered, as if a ghostly hand had touched my shoulder. The hand of a fellow-soldier.

'You'll do,' said de Poulengy, grinning. 'Now put on the swordbelt.'

I strapped on the swordbelt, gathering myself in at the waist. 'No, no.' De Poulengy held out his hand. 'It should rest light on your hip. There,' he said, adjusting the belt and tugging the loop for the sword into place. He held out the cuirass, a metal breastplate. 'Now this.'

I gave a grunt, then held out my arms straight while he strapped me into the breastplate, but as he stood back, I wrenched open the straps and threw it across the room.

'Wha—?' said de Poulengy, and I growled, rapidly tapping myself under the armpits, to show where the armour, badly shaped for a woman's chest, constricted and chafed. '*Bon Dieu!*' he said, clapping his hand to his brow. He retrieved the armour, saying, 'You'd better try the sword. If you use it, remember to pull it out afterwards.'

I growled furiously—did he think I was such an idiot? When he offered me the sword, I refused it and pushed it away, then again, until I had convinced him that I would never use it.

'Very well,' he said, huffily. 'I'll get you a pole-axe. It's the nearest we have to a quarterstaff.'

We mounted up. As we were about to leave, de Poulengy handed me a knife. 'You will need a blade, if only for self-defence. Stick that in your belt and when the time comes, *use* it.'

*   *   *

Jehanne stood alone at the city side of the fort. A silent crowd stood under the city walls, either side of the gate, which was closed. In her silver armour, proudly upright on her gleaming black destrier, she was a warrior queen. She turned to look as de Poulengy and I rode up and her white and gold standard streamed out its own challenge. Her confident smile was a blessing and I closed my eyes and thanked God for it.

'Wait here with the horses.' Jehanne dismounted and handed her reins to de Poulengy. He bowed, held out his arm to help me dismount, then took my reins too. 'Still no word from Talbot?' she asked him.

'Nothing.'

'Then I shall speak to Glasdale.' She took her standard in her right hand and set off towards the bastille. I hurried to join her. I tried to keep up with Jehanne's bold stride and, after a couple of stumbles, found the trick of it. Wearing armour is all about balance. You hold its weight on either shoulder, so you must stand as straight as a staff. I swung my right hand in time to my steps, but with my left gripped the pole-axe I had been given, wishing I had brought a shield. A pole-axe would not fend off arrows.

Jehanne's gaze was fixed on the fort ahead. Mine was everywhere. On either side of us the brown river flowed languidly in the soft afternoon light. Behind us the crowd was still. Ahead of us loomed the grey stone walls of the fort. English flags flew from each of the two towers. Were the enemy watching us? My ears were pricked for the thwang of longbows.

As we drew close to Les Tourelles, I heard men shouting and cheering. We came to the bulwark, a wall of stones held together with sunbaked clay, at the end of the bridge. Jehanne climbed it and stood on top, holding the standard. Praying for our safety, I pushed my pole-axe aside and scrambled up to her. 'Hooray!' came the shout. 'Hooray!'

There were no English in sight, but we could hear their cheers. Then an object flew high into the air, above the parapet that linked the two towers.

'God help us! What are they doing?'

It was obvious to me. They were playing a game, a ball game. Secure in their fort, they didn't even mount sentries. Had they seen us? Did they know we were here? 'Hooray! Hooray!' they cheered, absorbed in their game.

Furious tears filled Jehanne's eyes. She gave me the standard, cupped her hands round her mouth and yelled. 'Glas-dale! Glas-dale!'

Someone appeared on the parapet. 'It's the milkmaid!' shouted the man and there was rude laughter, then he disappeared. The English resumed their game.

'Glas-dale!' she called. 'Go home to your own country!' She waited.

'Hooray!' the men cheered.

'Leave France and get back to England! Leave France!'

Someone came to the parapet. 'Leave the bridge, milkmaid!' I could see from his livery that it was Glasdale.

For a long minute, Jehanne and he stared at each other, then a second man appeared and stood next to the first.

Jehanne shouted to them. 'I come to do you great damage. Leave France!'

'I shall leave France, indeed I shall! But before I leave, France will be ours!' His voice carried across the water like a clarion call.

More men gathered behind him, fanning out along the parapet.

'Glas-dale! Go home and I shall spare your life!'

'You go home!' There were shouts and catcalls. 'Leave soldiering to the men!' Glasdale bellowed.

'Never!'

'If I catch you, witch, I shall burn you.'

'God help you, Glas-dale!' shouted Jehanne. With her eyes closed, she tilted her head right back so that she looked straight up at the sky. Slowly she lowered her head and looked straight at the man opposite.

'You shall die in battle. You shall die steeped in your sins. God will not forgive you!'

Jehanne turned from them and jumped down from the bulwark. I lowered the standard then climbed down.

Out of sight of the English, Jehanne had dropped to her knees and buried her face in her hands.

'*Père au ciel . . . Mon Père . . . Père,*' she called, beseeching God to hear, but the rest of her prayer was lost in an outburst of weeping.

What could I do? I knelt with her and silently prayed, '*With respect, Lord, I sincerely hope that You know what You are doing.*'

When Jehanne recovered, she wiped her face, leaving it streaked with grime. 'He said he'd burn me—' she sniffed and scrambled to her feet. 'He'll have to catch me first!'

CHAPTER EIGHTEEN
A DISCOVERY

The crowds by the walls came to greet us as we arrived at the city after our long march back over the bridge. They cheered and called out their usual cry: *'La Pucelle*!' to which they now added: 'Scourge of the English!' They had watched us climb the bulwark and seen Jehanne's standard fly in the wind, but they had not witnessed our humiliation and assumed our safe return was a victory. Their cries followed us to our lodgings. All the way my back prickled with fear. Marching across the bridge from Les Tourelles, with Jehanne going ahead, I had expected the thud of an English arrow between my shoulder blades. I was shaking. I was afraid. If I was afraid how could I be a true warrior?

For three days I waited for the call to arms. We were at stalemate. Dunois went back to Blois with Jehanne's men to collect more provisions. In his absence, Jehanne reconnoitred all the English positions on a long ride around the city. She rode, battle-ready, with her standard held high, followed by hordes of cheering citizens. Fully armed, I rode by her side. The English ignored her. Not a shot, neither arrow nor missile, was fired.

Her followers took this for a sign that the English were

powerless to hurt her, but I knew they were wrong. The enemy saw her as an amusement: she was no threat to them.

While we waited, more and more troops crept into Orléans, by day and night, along the unguarded eastern roads. On the third day Dunois sent news that he was approaching the city with supplies. The English were beginning to take notice. Their reinforcements were on their way to the forts, from the north. But when Jehanne and I rode out, with five hundred men, to accompany the supplies into the city, there was no sign of the enemy. They let us pass. The English continued their waiting game.

Once Dunois was back in Orléans the sense of delay was stifling. People openly clamoured for action. All morning Dunois stayed closeted with his captains. Jehanne went to pray in the cathedral. After lunch she went to sleep quietly and, fearful, I polished my gear. It was hard to breathe: the air seemed heavily charged, as if brewing a storm.

A thought grew into a conviction: I should not be afraid of battle, because I was the daughter of a royal chevalier.

I took my father's box from my pack. Carefully I opened it and unwrapped my inheritance: the badge, the missal, and the glove.

I studied the badge, which gave me my father's name: de Louvier. De Louvier. It was a proud name and I still had unfinished business with my uncle, Sir Gaston. I would not let him stay free. I would not. There was a debt to be paid.

I picked up my father's glove. My thoughts flew to the day of his death on the field of Agincourt, and I imagined the sounds of that conflict, the shouts of the soldiers and the whinnying of horses, their hooves stamping the ground, and the hissing flight of a thousand deadly arrows.

Père, I called. *Mon père. Let me be as brave a warrior as you were when I enter the field.* I brushed away flakes of mud and pressed my hand on top of the glove: it was the same size and shape. Then I put my hand into my father's glove and fitted my fingers into the places where his fingers had been. It was a perfect fit. Almost. I took out my hand.

Right at the end of the forefinger was a stone, or something like a stone, something hard and round. I squeezed and stretched the end of the leather finger until the stone moved a little way down, then pressed and shook the glove hard, until finally the object was dislodged and fell into the palm of my hand.

Daubed with clay—deliberately?—I knew at once what it was: glints of gold showed through the soil. I rubbed off as much as I could, then washed it in water.

It was my father's ring! Impressed on the boss was the family emblem, two wide chevrons on a round. The de Louvier seal.

Suddenly an alarm call shrieked in the street. Jehanne sprang to the window and called down for news. 'Saint Loup!' was the cry. 'The people have attacked Saint Loup!' The English fort to the east of the city.

I pushed the seal back into its hiding place, packed my box, and shoved it to the bottom of my bag.

'Saddle my horse,' Jehanne called to the page below, then turned back into the room. 'Help me get into my armour.'

We helped each other, then ran downstairs to the horses,

and were soon ready to fly to the attack. As we left the stable yard, Jehanne's brother, Pierre, stuck his head out of our window. 'Here!' he cried, handing down her furled standard.

'Saint Loup!' she called to him.

'I'll be there!' he said, as the banner unfurled around her, like the wing of a great bird.

We made for the eastern gate, hindered by the crowds rallying to the battle call. Men and women, young and old, poured forth. Great cheers erupted as Jehanne rode past. At the gate we met porters already bringing back wounded. Jehanne leaned down to speak to a groaning man on a litter, then threw back her head and cried, 'This is French blood they're spilling. *Allons . . . frères! Par Dieu! Allons y!*' Her banner held aloft, she galloped out of Orléans.

The road to the fort was lit by hundreds of bobbing torches, as men hurried to the fight, on horse or on foot, arming themselves as they went. Jehanne found a way through them and forged ahead, leaving me caught in the throng. I had never seen so many soldiers as were heading for the bastille: on the road we crowded together, so that our horses banged sides or were caught in a knot of people, hampering our own progress. Slowly I rode on, trying to keep sight of Jehanne's now tiny figure and the fluttering standard that streamed out behind her.

Before long I made out the silhouette of the church at Saint Loup, around which the English had constructed their fort. The story was that a party of citizens had attacked it, without consulting the captains.

As we got closer I caught battle sound: men shouting, the clash of weapons, the noises of dogs and horses, and the sudden blast from a culverin, a small cannon, to break down the walls. My senses fired, as if I had swallowed saltpetre—I can find no better way to describe it. My doubts fled. I roared and edged my way into a gap, then kicked my heels into Lionheart's flanks and galloped towards the fray.

Almost at once, I was closed in again. 'Back! Back!' shouted a man, a chevalier by the look of his fancy accoutrements, forcing his way to the front. My battle thirst faded as I obeyed. As he passed, the man used his horse's shoulder to shove me aside. I shoved back, but, wrong-footed, Lionheart stumbled and, with a growl of annoyance, I had to cede my place, and found myself in the field alongside the road, with the other squires.

'Mariane!' Pierre rode up behind me. 'Where's Jehanne?'

Dieu. The incident with the knight had distracted me and I had lost sight of her. I stood up in my stirrups to find her and saw the standard, a small white sign in the darkness, way ahead. She had almost reached the bastille. Pierre followed my gaze and saw it too. Together we galloped to join her.

Inside the bastille, the fight raged. Outside, scaling ladders had been put to the walls, and our men flooded up, drew swords, then with great shouts, plunged over into the thick of it.

At the foot of the wall, some ladders lay broken and discarded, pushed from the walls by the English defenders, and men lay where they had fallen, like rag puppets, some wounded, some dead.

My first instinct was to dismount, to cover the dead and tend the wounded, but I steeled myself to look away, as Jehanne, with Dunois and the other captains, urged us to climb the wall with them and join the fight within the bastille.

When a trumpet signalled the arrival of English reinforcements, we did not falter. As I reached the top of the ladder, I heard the noise of the two armies meeting on the road and crashing together like pans in a barrel.

I pulled myself on to the top of the wall, steadied myself between two stones, then leapt down on to the wooden platform below. The church stood at the heart of the fort, surrounded by high wooden walls, buttressed with packed earth. Between these defences and the church was a gap of twenty feet, thronged with men fighting. On the steps leading down from the platform stood one or two French, with drawn swords, keeping watch as our soldiers streamed over and leapt into the fray.

There the fighting was grim and furious. Someone behind me barked: '*Avance! Pousse-toi!*' so I gathered myself and jumped down into a snarling hell.

I fell badly and crouched, looking up at a mass of faces, red with sweat and blood. I was deafened by the ring of steel on armour, the grunts and shouts of men, and I flinched at the screams of victims as blades bit.

Eeling my way to a space at the foot of the outer wall, I lay with my back against it as if I were wounded, then saw Jehanne's standard, planted in the middle of the enclosure. There was no sign of her, but, like God's own breath, the wind swelled the banner. There was no one near it, so I stood up and walked towards it, keeping my eyes on the fluttering golden lilies of France.

Someone thumped me hard in the back and I fell forward, one hand pressed to the ground. I turned to see a blade swing past me, within a hair's breadth. My assailant, a well-armed English soldier, swung the sword back again, but it fell limp from his hand before it reached me when a Frenchman struck the top of his sword arm. I heard the bone crack and the man wailed and fell to the ground.

My rescuer next caught a blow that brought him to his knees in front of me. 'S'cours!' he hissed, his neck spurting blood. I hesitated—then drew my knife.

As an Englishman stood over my friend to deliver his coup de grâce, I sprang up, jabbed the blade under his guard and thrust it home to the hilt.

The knife jerked from my grasp as he fell, and the fight, like some monstrous creature, floundered around us as I bent over his body. Remembering de Poulengy's injunction, I concentrated on getting a firm grip on the knife in order to pull it out.

I tugged, then tugged again, and at last pulled it free, and the man groaned and rolled over, curling himself up. Then he coughed, just once, and lay still.

I turned back to the soldier I had tried to save, but he also lay dead, his body soaked in his blood. Nausea rocked me. What good had I done? Using both hands, I wiped the blade on my tunic, then threaded it back in my belt, but all the while I was telling myself I would fight no more.

'Mariane!' De Poulengy, his face urgent and strained, fended off blows with his sword. He held up a pole-axe.

He glanced at my face, then at the man at my feet, but he threw the weapon anyway, and I caught it. *'Avance!'* he called, jerking his head forward. 'Get on with it!'

It was the spur I needed. I found the weapon's point of balance and holding it centred before me stood to the attack. And I knew, as all true soldiers do that, come flood, come fire, come hell itself, I must fight on or die.

CHAPTER NINETEEN
I RENEW AN ACQUAINTANCE

The fight lasted for three hours, then suddenly it was over. Trumpets sounded the call to put up our weapons. I lowered my pole-axe, wiped the sweat from my brow and, gasping for breath, watched the remaining English being taken prisoner. Some would have killed them on the spot, but Jehanne forebade such cold-blooded slaughter and they were sent as prisoners into the city.

The men whooped and shouted their victory: they had captured a fort, they had turned back an army of six hundred English sent to defend it, and they had prisoners to bargain with. Defiant, full of spirit, they marched into Orléans and burst on to the streets, singing and dancing. The prisoners, bound, stood in a small sullen crowd in the market place. Some spat at them and threw rotten food. Jehanne rode between the prisoners and the crowd, giving orders that the English be treated decently. She asked us to pray for them and for the unshriven dead, of both sides. She urged us to confess our sins and cleanse our souls.

On the day after, being a holy day for both sides, there would be no fighting. I was glad of the rest, a little time to tend aching muscles, time to reflect on my new status as a soldier, marked by first blood.

Truthfully, my mind tormented me with it, repeating over and over the scene of my first kill. I attended Mass with Jehanne, then afterwards, returned with her to our lodging. Perhaps I could distract myself, I thought, by showing her the seal that I had found. Perhaps I could seek her advice.

A friend followed us in from the street. 'La Hire!' Jehanne threw her arms round the man who stood before us. Over her shoulder his eyes smiled a greeting and I grinned back. La Hire. He had the heart of a bear, the eye of a hawk, and a giant's strength in his right arm. We had first met at the dauphin's court. I knew he had been sent to Orléans, to harry the forts to the north. This was our first time of meeting since we had left Chinon.

He drew back, then dropped to one knee and bowed his head. 'My lady,' he said.

'Get up, la Hire!' said Jehanne. 'There'll be no "my ladying". Where have you been? Tell me the news.'

As we walked into the house, I sensed la Hire draw away from us. Other captains arrived, crossed the hall and went into the salon. Men's voices greeted him. 'La Hire! *Viens-toi* . . . come on!' With an apology, la Hire left us standing in the hall.

'Who's here?' said Jehanne, on her way up the stairs. I shrugged and she came back down. She went to the door of the salon, knocked and entered. I followed.

Dunois sat at the head of a long table, his captains ranged either side. La Hire was just taking his place.

'What's this, Dunois?' said Jehanne. 'A war council? Why did you not tell me?'

Motioning his captains to remain seated, Dunois stood up and came round the table. 'A useful victory at Saint Loup, my dear, but now we have to decide the next move.'

'Of course. That's why I should be here.'

'Your presence is not required.'

'Mind your words. I bring you the counsel of God, which is better than any.'

The men exchanged meaningful glances.

'Jehanne,' said Dunois, pulling out a chair. 'Please sit down.'

'I will not,' she replied.

'Then at least hear the plan.'

'Very well.'

'Tomorrow we attack the English headquarters at St Laurent, with our whole force.'

Jehanne looked scornfully round the table.

'Messires, you will fail. The next move must be against Glasdale at Les Tourelles. A child can see it. Do you think the garrison there will sit playing dice while you attack St Laurent? We control the whole of the east. We move north or south. South is less well-defended and the nearest and best prize is Les Tourelles. St Laurent? Are you mad? It lies within shouting distance of two . . . three . . .' She gazed up at the ceiling, as she counted. 'Four well-garrisoned forts. Now tell me the real plan.'

The captains muttered. Some smiled. Dunois sighed. 'We attack St Laurent with sufficient force to draw out the Tourelles garrison then, when they have crossed the Loire, we send out a second contingent to attack Les Tourelles as we please.'

'As God pleases,' said Jehanne.

As we entered our room, Jehanne, stifling her anger, burst out, 'I must ask for counsel,' and flung herself down on her knees in front of the cross, which she had set up on a shelf near the bed.

I went to sit quietly at the other end of the room, watching and wondering, as always, how she could turn in an instant from high agitation to complete unbreakable stillness.

We were so different. She, single-minded, her whole being fixed on God; me, many-minded, too frantic to hear His voice, my thoughts darting like a caged bird from one point of anguish to another.

I unpacked my box and took out the de Louvier seal. I put it on the forefinger of my right hand and thought of Sir Gaston, my mother's murderer, and my private vow to avenge her death. After Saint Loup I felt weak, empty of rage. To kill again, to do the deed, I must find the soldier within me, that core of steel that would strengthen my heart as I plunged home the knife. A flood of horror rose up and threatened to black out my mind, but I looked at Jehanne and held firm, fixing my thoughts on our last meeting with Sir Gaston. He had said we would meet again in Orléans. So where was he?

'Mariane,' called Jehanne, standing up. 'I must send the English another message.' I reached for my writing gear.

'Begin in the usual way, then write this: "The King of

Heaven commands you to abandon your forts and go back where you belong. If you fail to do this, I, Jehanne la Pucelle, will make such *brouhaha* as will be remembered forever. This is my last message. I shall not write any more."'

As I sanded the ink, she said, 'Add this—"Send back my herald and I will send you some of the prisoners taken at Saint Loup." *Bien* . . . it's finished.'

She watched me roll up the letter, then said, 'Put on your armour. Come with me. Let's deliver the message.'

The wind was brisk as Jehanne and I rode again to the bridge across the Loire, which led to the fort of Les Tourelles. A crowd accompanied us to the city gate, chattering about the previous day's battle, still elated, attributing the victory to Jehanne. Some came close, reaching out to touch her armour and I realized that they believed she had a mysterious power, which might pass into them and heal all their ills. I tried to stop them touching her, but Jehanne neither encouraged nor discouraged them. Did she even notice? As always her purpose was fixed, her eyes on the bastille, her pace steady.

As we approached the bastille, all was quiet. We saw no one except four sentries facing the bridge, as still as painted effigies. The English flag flapped in the breeze from the river and a thread of smoke rose above one of the two towers.

'Dinner time,' smiled Jehanne.

'Or a late breakfast.'

'Or *sieste*,' she said. Her eyes twinkled. 'Let's wake them up.'

She took out the letter, turned to the small crowd who had followed us and pointed. 'You there, with the bow. Can you use it?'

'I can, sire! I mean, my lady!' replied a squire, dressed in a blue cloak, with a fine black leather bonnet pulled low over his brow. He stepped forward and gave a low bow. The crowd tittered at his mistake and the boy, his face flushed, swung round to scowl at them.

'Call me Jehanne.'

He turned back.

'At your pleasure, my lady,' he said.

'He has courtly manners,' Jehanne whispered to me, smiling. 'Tie this letter to one of your arrows,' she said and the boy did so. 'Now shoot and send it straight to the English.'

The boy took up his position, raised his bow and drew back the string, sighting a line along his forefinger. He loosed the arrow which soared in a high arc across the gap between the bridge and Les Tourelles.

Jehanne cupped her mouth in her hands. 'Glas-dale! Read! Here's news for you!'

'News from the dauphin's whore!' retorted one of the English guards fouling our French tongue with his vile words. Praise God, Jehanne, congratulating the archer, didn't hear.

As we progressed back to the city Jehanne went ahead to a meeting with Pasquerel her confessor and I found myself walking alongside our archer friend. Side-glances told me that he was in the service of someone of high rank. Then he tugged off his bonnet.

'You don't reco'nize me, do yer? I reco'nized you straight away.'

I grasped the stranger's sleeve and pulled him round until we were face to face. Beneath the long hair and the weatherworn face was Didier. Was he now squire to Sir Gaston?

'Still dumb, lame-brain?' he said with a grin, then he punched me in the shoulder, but I was too quick for him and my wrists are as strong as steel. Grinning back, I clamped my right hand over his forearm, lifting it up and pushing it back until he lost his balance.

'Or' right, calm down. Pax, pax.' I let him go. 'That's me bow arm, an' all, innit?' he said. I shrugged and put my arm round his shoulder and gave him a manly hug, then poked my finger in his ribs and spread my hand to ask where he had been. We set off walking again.

'Where I've been? Yer'll never guess. I been to La Paix. Yeah. Like I told yer, at Chinon, Sir Gaston giv' the order. "Saddle the 'orse, Didier. We're goin' 'ome, to La Paix." An' we did, an' all.'

As we reached the end of the bridge and separated to take different ways, I slapped his arm to make him stay and tell me more.

'More? Tell yer what. What yer doin' tonight? After arms practice and prayers, o' course.' I laughed out loud with pleasure at meeting up with Didier again. 'Meet me at the Grapes, then. D'yer know it? At dusk. We'll talk then, at least I will. You'll just 'ave to listen, lame- brain.'

He winked at me and I tried to swagger and wink back, but could only manage to blink both eyes at once, as if I had sand in them. Didier raised his eyebrows to heaven, then turned off to his road, leaving me to take mine.

CHAPTER TWENTY
THE GRAPES

It was already dark when I arrived at the tavern and shoved my way through the noisy crowd at the door. The Grapes was a popular venue, it seemed, especially when there was a victory to celebrate.

Self-conscious, I stood on the threshold. Except for two serving-girls, this was the men's domain, a drinking place for the rough and tumble of soldiers. Here were no captains, only men of the rank and file, a couple of squires, some lads and runabouts.

I stepped forward, recognizing many faces and, with brief nods, I acknowledged their greetings and realized that I had nothing to fear. They knew me as Mariane, a girl in a soldier's dress; their eyes looked at me briefly, then slid away. I was friend, not foe; someone they could turn their back on without hazard.

I scanned each table, searching for Didier, and there he was, hidden behind a settle, in a far corner away from the fire, so much quieter and more private. He signalled and I raised my hand, then threaded my way through the crowd to join him.

'Yer late,' he announced, 'I've already bottomed this jug.' He lifted the wine jar and tipped it upside down, spilling a few drops. 'Well met, anyway.' He slid round the table to make room and I sat opposite. Across the board, we clasped forearms briefly in greeting. 'Well met, lame-brain.' He smiled and with a new look of respect, mur-mured, 'Mariane.'

I picked up the empty jug and caught the eye of the serving-girl.

Didier leaned forward, then put his elbows on the table. 'So, what do you make of Orléans? It's a long way from 'ome, I can tell you. Where you from, Mariane? Reims, innit? I'm from Paris meself.' *Reims*. He knew my name and where I was from. Did he know who my father was? Did he know about the will and about La Paix?

Didier was Sir Gaston's man. I pressed my lips tight shut. By sound or gesture, I must not betray that I had the de Louvier seal.

'Me mother's a laundress, in a big 'ouse. She were that proud when I got took on by Sir Gaston. There's eleven of us, see? Six girls and five lads. Sir Gaston used to visit up at the 'ouse, and one day she came straight out and asked 'im if 'e could do with a decent lad, 'ard-workin', clean, all 'is own teef, no great happetite. That was a lie! I've always been a good eater, ferocious. An' do you know what 'e said? 'E said yes! She were delighted.

''E started me off in the stable like, shovellin' muck— no 'arm in that, builds up yer muscles—and I got on so well that now I'm a de Louvier squire.'

Did he expect me to start when he said the name? He flicked open his cloak and studied the de Louvier device on his tunic, pulling it straight, as if it were still a surprise to him. He glanced at me, but I kept my face blank and sipped my wine. My skin felt hot. Was I blushing?

'Tell yer what, though, between you and me, I'm goin'

back to Paris, when this lot's over. Sir Gaston's a hard man.' Didier drew in a short sharp breath. 'To be truthful, I 'ate him. I 'ate what he does. There's that beautiful place, La Paix. Like I said, we've just come from there. Well, when I first saw it I thought it were fit for God Allmighty 'isself. Like a 'eavenly palace, it is. The 'ouse, all carved stone, shining gold from ever so far away. You see it shining on the 'orizon, and it seems to call out to you, draw you to it, like, as if it's a safe 'aven. And it was for the first hour or so. Then 'e starts, Sir Gaston. 'onest, Mariane, I thought a demon 'ad took 'old of 'im. La Paix is in the hands of the church, you know, until the old master's heir shows up?' His voice lifted as if asking a question. 'The old master, Sir François de Louvier?' Again the question. He looked at me and waited. I kept my thoughts to myself.

'Seems 'e left the whole lot to his mistress Eloise, and after her, to their child. Sir Gaston's like a man possessed about the inheritance. This child, a girl, has the family seal, see, the old master's signet ring. There's no will, so if Sir Gaston could get hold of it, he could mebbe get La Paix for 'isself. 'E's desperate to find this seat.' He sipped his wine and looked at me again over the rim of his cup. 'Desperate.' Again the pause. 'Anyway, back to La Paix. The prior—'im what's in charge now—was most 'ospitable. Nothing was too much trouble. We 'ad the best beds, best wine and vittles, and a tour of the estate. There are fields full of apple trees there, so full o' blossom you could swoon from the scent, and bees, in dozens of 'ives under the trees, and ponds, crammed full o' pike. And proper gardens, round the 'ouse, wiv the plants laid out in their proper beds round the well, some for med'cine, some for scent, some for dyein'. Like Heaven itself. Byootiful. But when I said as much to Sir Gaston, 'is face went black as thunder, and 'e starts shouting that if 'e couldn't have La Paix, then no one would: 'e would see to it that the whole lot was burned, razed to the ground first. I ask you, what sort o' man would do that?'

I shook my head. Didier frowned and fixed his eyes on a spot over my left shoulder.

'We went to see 'is sister,' he went on. 'A lovely woman, tall and beautiful and serene as moonlight. Very devout, you can sense these fings. She's still grieving for 'er 'usband, killed in the war. She works as a healer in the infirmary attached to the priory. I fink all her time is spent in 'ealing and praying, praying and 'ealing. She's a good woman, but what does Sir Gaston do? 'E gives orders for 'er to be beaten for what she done, upholding her brother François's wishes about the estate. 'E 'ad 'er taken to the cellar and beaten! I was there. She took twenty strokes and she never uttered a sound. It was me what felt sick.

'I tell you the man has a demon inside 'im. Between you and me—' Didier leaned towards me and lowered his voice. '—I shall leave when this lot's done. I'll go to Paris. I can blink out o' sight there, like a snuffed candle. 'e'll never find me.'

He put down his cup and held it with both hands. 'If I were this girl, if I 'ad the seal, I would make 'aste to La Paix and stake my claim, as soon as I could.' His eyes asked me the question. *Do you have the seal?* I sipped my wine. Could I trust him?

'As I said,' he went on, pouring wine into both our cups,

'Sir Gaston is looking for the seal and Gawd 'elp this girl if she does 'ave the seal and Sir Gaston finds 'er.' There was a long pause, then he said, 'I should like 'er to know, that she 'as a friend in Didier, whom she may trust wiv 'er life, if ever need arise.'

He drained his wine cup, then after a pause during which he looked both bashful and earnest, he said, 'How's fings wiv the Maid? She's a rare wonder, isn't she? Do you know,' he said, 'I've never truly felt French before, but now I do. She's cleared my mind on the subject. These English should leave, cousins or not. We should each stick to our own country. France for the French!'

I lifted my cup and we drank the pledge.

'So,' Didier went on, 'we attack again in the morning. You're close to the Maid—what are the plans?'

I picked up a handful of sand from the floor and scattered it on the table, then drew the distinctive outline of two towers.

'Les Tourelles,' Didier whispered. I nodded. 'Makes sense. That's the obvious target.'

We drank on, settling into a companionable and sleepy silence, which was rudely broken when a gang of fine boys at the next table started to sing 'La Belle Suzette' to the landlady's daughter, who flicked up her skirt and began to dance.

'Look a' that,' muttered Didier, his head swaying. As the crowd pushed back to make room for the dancing girl, he put down his cup, twisted in his seat and sat, legs apart, leaning forward to watch.

'You got a friend, Mariane?' he said, as the dancing finished.

I shook my head.

'Wha', a pretty girl like you? I bet the lads run after you like ducks off a pond.'

I blushed crimson, then cursed myself. Luckily Didier's attention was drawn to the door which swung wide to admit a newcomer. A figure stood on the threshold. I looked at him in his black cloak and knew instantly who it was.

'*Dieu!* Sir Gaston,' said Didier. 'I wasn't expectin' 'im till the mornin'. 'E told me to wait in his lodgings.'

Sir Gaston was moving from table to table. 'Get up,' Didier hissed. 'Go out the back. Now!' Pulling my cloak round me, I slipped out of the back door into the cold night air. Didier followed. As he muttered goodnight and turned to leave, I put my hand on his arm.

''S awright,' he whispered. 'I'll tell 'im I went out gatherin' information. 'E'll like that. I'll tell 'im about Les Tourelles. Thanks, Mariane.' He touched my hand, then set off down the dark alley.

I watched until he turned the corner at the end, joining a crowd on the street, then made my way back to my lodging.

CHAPTER TWENTY-ONE
'AVANCE! AVANCE!'

Early the next day we went to meet Dunois and the other captains. All glanced at us as we entered the crowded salon.

As Jehanne went to Dunois, I went to the window and pushed the shutter aside. Hundreds of soldiers were massing in the square. Armed and purposeful, they formed ranks facing the road that led to the eastern gate. The army was ready. The drum sounded. They set off at a steady pace.

We would attack Les Tourelles. The English surely felt secure in the fort with two towers, which seemed impregnable. The break in the bridge prevented attack from the northern side; the south was defended by the Loire itself. Beyond the river was an earthwork and ditch. Beyond that, another fort: the Bastille des Augustins. We must take Les Augustins first, then claim the earthwork, under enemy fire. The English position seemed unassailable, but we must take it if we were to win Orléans.

I flexed my right hand, in my father's glove, now gleaming with the fat that I had rubbed into the leather to make it supple again. On my right forefinger, I wore the de Louvier seal—I would die defending it.

I rubbed my thumb over its shape. I would kill Sir

Gaston; that was justice. His life for my mother's. But in battle you had to kill and kill again. Boys, men, strangers. Innocent or guilty, they were the enemy. Kill or be killed. That was war.

'What's this?' Jehanne stabbed at a map. De Poulengy looked at it over her shoulder. 'It's another blessed fort. *Saint . . . Jean . . . le . . . Blanc.*'

'It's between us and Les Augustins.'

'Then we deal with it first,' said Dunois.

'It's lightly manned, should be easy meat, hardly worth breaking a sweat for,' said la Hire with a grin.

'None of the forts will be won easily. Don't be too confident.'

'What's the plan, then?' said la Hire.

'We attack from the east and the south.' Dunois traced the route on the map. 'We ford the river, using the island as a base, and muster on the south bank. La Hire, you're in charge of the crossing. Pray for good wind and water. It won't be easy.'

'Then we'd better begin!' La Hire put on his helmet and moved to the door. Dunois stood in his way.

'I want you and Jehanne to lead the men out of the city and down to the river, without haste, in good order. Supervise the crossing.'

'And once we reach the south bank?' said la Hire.

'We attack Saint Jean le Blanc.'

'Jehanne,' Dunois said, 'stay to the last man, then go yourself to the south bank and supervise the crossing from there. When they attack the forts, stay back. Let the men take Saint Jean and Les Augustins. Don't risk yourself. Let them clear the way for us to Les Tourelles.

De Poulengy, keep those culverin dry, and out of sight. I want those to be a surprise.'

Culverin fired stone balls, as big as a fist. They prove useful against stone walls.

Crowds lined the ramparts as we left Orléans, cheering and waving shirts and aprons, as if the victory were already ours. Their faith fired my own and I sat straighter on Lionheart, head held high.

The light wind, the bright day, breathed a victory, not only in the battle for Les Tourelles, but for Orléans and for France itself. If there were ever a marker on time's clock, to say 'This is the hour', I saw it then, in the proud pennons of the captains, in the ranks of marching soldiers, in the sight of Jehanne in her gleaming armour, with her flying standard, Jehanne the Maid, Daughter of God, at whose side I rode into battle.

We watched the last of the men make the crossing, then dismounted and walked our steeds into the boats. The ferrymen rowed us across the Loire and set us down on the island, then we crossed to the southern side via a 'bridge' made from two boats tied together. It rocked alarmingly as I led Lionheart over it.

Our army poured over the Loire in a steady stream and went straight to attack the fort at St Jean le Blanc. Jehanne stood on the south bank like a figurehead, her white and gold banner signalling its call to arms. As the men passed they beat their swords on their breastplates. Lionheart reared and whinnied loudly, startled by the noise.

We were standing watching the march, when a distant trumpet sounded from the head of the column. I stood up in my stirrups to look. La Hire was galloping back.

'Saint Jean le Blanc's deserted!' he called. 'They've retired to Les Augustins!'

Jehanne spurred her horse to the fort and I followed.

From the ramparts of Saint Jean le Blanc, we looked out at the Bastille des Augustins, half a mile distant. An English trumpet call from the bastille sounded the signal to retire. A small dustcloud showed where the last of their soldiers from Saint Jean le Blanc were racing to reach the gates before they were closed against us.

In the fields behind us, the men stood, uncertain. What now? Should they go on to Les Augustins? When Dunois appeared, Jehanne climbed down to speak to him.

With a sharp tug of the reins, Dunois brought his horse to a halt.

'Why did you not wait? I ordered you to stay back.' His face was dark with ill temper.

'The English are on the run. We have them! We must attack Les Augustins.'

'You must obey my orders!'

'We must all obey God!' Jehanne mounted her horse. Another trumpet call cut off their argument. Dunois gestured angily to la Hire. 'See what's happening!'

Shading his eyes, la Hire looked out at Les Augustins. 'The English are coming,' he said. 'They're on the attack.'

'And we're still crossing the river,' Dunois said. 'We must retreat.'

'No!' said Jehanne.

She made a grab for Dunois's reins, but he pulled them out of her grasp. 'We retreat. We re-group and come at them, in good order, at a better time.'

Jehanne gasped. 'We lose our advantage!'

'Sound the retreat!' Dunois called to the trumpeter. The soldiers started to turn. La Hire jumped from the ramparts. 'If we're leaving, we'd better leave now,' he said, scrambling on to his horse.

Dunois galloped back to the crossing place, shouting his orders. Jehanne's horse twisted and turned, but she did not follow Dunois.

'I must attack!' she said as if to herself. Then out loud, with a flourish of her standard, 'We attack! Follow me when you can!' She set off alone to meet the English.

La Hire caught my eye and raised his eyebrows. He couched his lance. I drew my sword. La Hire's horse reared as he looked over his shoulder at the retreating army. 'The Maid attacks! Don't leave her to fight alone! *Avance!*' he cried. '*Avance!*'

'*Avance!*' The cry passed like fire through the ranks. A thousand retreating soldiers hesitated, then one by one, they turned back to the fort. '*Avance!*' cried la Hire. '*Avance!*' A thousand men broke ranks and ran to us. We spurred our mounts to follow Jehanne to the Bastille des Augustins. A thousand swords followed.

At the sight of our army advancing, with Jehanne flying out in front, the English turned tail and fled, dropping weapons and gear, scuffling in the dust, barging each other aside to reach safety. As the last man entered, the gates of the Bastille des Augustins shut with an iron clang.

They were not safe for long. Dunois and the rest of the army joined us. The soldiers still on the island ignored the ferries and plunged into the Loire to reach the fight. We threw our ladders against the walls of the fort and, with the advantage of surprise, flooded over the ramparts.

Even with our greater numbers, it took all day to take the bastille. The English had a champion who killed many of our men and repelled all attack. He was a giant of a man, a warrior whose strength seemed unquenchable. But when the culverineer brought up his weapon, the big Englishman fell at last, stopped by the cannon's stone fist.

Was it this that made them lose heart? The English sounded the retreat and left the fort as best they could, heading for Les Tourelles. La Hire and the others would have hounded them to the earthwork, but Dunois ordered the call to retire and lay down our weapons. The day was won.

Rejoicing, we moved out of Les Augustins, taking with us the supplies left by the English, then set fire to the fort as a sign of our intent to the enemy, now entrenched in their last hiding place, their stronghold on the bridge, Les Tourelles.

Another fire flamed up that night, from the last fort in the west. 'St Prive! St Prive!' came the cry. That was when the English finally abandoned their positions on the south side of the Loire. That night the whole of the south bank became ours.

We made camp outside Les Augustins, posting sentries to watch Les Tourelles. Jehanne wanted to spend the night there, with the rest, but she had taken a foot wound, from a caltrop, a spiked iron ball, one of dozens littering the ditch outside the fort, and was persuaded to rest safely back in the city.

'Tomorrow . . .' she murmured, as we headed back for the crossing. 'Glasdale thinks he sits safely within Les Tourelles. Not for much longer.'

CHAPTER TWENTY-TWO
ENEMIES

When we returned to the city, Dunois called a meeting. The salon was crowded. Dunois stood facing la Hire at the head of the long table, which he thumped with his fist.

'We could have lost every advantage today, through your rashness. What were you thinking?' He looked at Jehanne. 'That the two of you alone could defeat the English?'

Defiant, la Hire glared at Dunois. 'We charged and they fled before us, like mist in the sun,' he said. 'You saw it yourself, you were there.'

Jehanne pushed her way forward.

'Admit it, Dunois,' said la Hire. 'What Jehanne says is true. She is the Maid, sent by God Himself. How can you deny it? Today God was with us. Jehanne is His scourge.'

'La Hire, la Hire.' From the back of the salon, a mocking voice cut through the argument. 'You were lucky. The gamble paid off, that's all. Come to your senses, man. "*Jehanne is His scourge?*" What nonsense is this? The girl has bewitched you.' Some of the captains gasped at this slur. I moved until I could see the speaker.

Sir Gaston de Louvier sat alone on a high-backed settle next to the fire. He leaned back at his ease, finely accoutred in mail, cuirasse, and greaves.

All fell silent. They were in awe of him, the dauphin's spymaster, afraid of the power over life and death that his rank commanded.

He stood up and I stepped back into the crowd to avoid his gaze.

'Be wary, all of you. There is madness abroad. This girl, dressed up as a man—' He gestured to Jehanne. '—has let it loose.'

Some of the captains baulked at his words. 'She's the Maid!' 'She's from God!' It was la Hire who turned to confront him. He held up his fingers, counting off our successes. 'Saint Loup, Saint Jean le Blanc, Les Augustins—we couldn't have done it without her.'

'Keep your head, la Hire. Don't be taken in by this myth. The Maid of Lorraine? A Divine Saviour? Stories and legends, my friend. But I don't deny that Jehanne la Pucelle is useful. Who would not be moved by the sight of a fearless French soldier, no bigger than a child, riding alone into terrible danger, scorning even to wear a helmet. She also has a trump card to play: she's not even trained for it, she's a girl, more suited to hearth and home than to the battlefield. Tricked out in her armour, she acts out her story and persuades gullible fools to follow her.'

'The people love her!'

'She will get them all killed.' He shot Jehanne a sharp glance. 'You claim to hear the voices of saints, to receive the pronouncements of God? I think not.'

There was uproar in the chamber. I put my hands over my ears to drown out the angry voices.

As Sir Gaston shook his head and seated himself again, Dunois called out with authority: 'Messires, messires. Sir

Gaston is welcome here. We have heard his opinion: you have your own. But one thing should be made clear. An army acts on its orders. There is a chain of command and I am at the head of it: I alone. Dunois. My orders are that we stay in Orléans, until we get reinforcements.'

La Hire burst out: 'But the way is clear to Les Tourelles—'

'I said no!' Dunois thundered.

All this time Jehanne had stood silent. Now she spoke. 'You still doubt me. You still doubt that God is with us, that I am the sign. Well, hear this. I shall not be with you for long. But my death day is not yet, though tomorrow, in battle, the blood will spurt from my body. I have already told you this, Dunois.' She touched her chest on the left hand side, between her shoulder and breast.

'There will be no battles tomorrow!'

'Do you think God follows your orders, Dunois?' Jehanne said gently, then she turned on her heel and left, saying, 'Good night. Good night to all of you.'

As I followed Jehanne from the room, Sir Gaston's voice rang out behind me. 'Wait!' I turned as he approached.

'Mariane!' he said, drawing me aside. 'It's good to see that you're safe.' I kept my face a blank. He reached down and lifted up my right hand. 'You have restored the glove. May it bring you better luck than it brought my poor brother.'

Sir Gaston twisted my hand over and clasped it with his right hand. 'He wore the seal here, right here.' He loosened his grip, then felt the leather along my forefinger. Our eyes locked as he felt the hard metal of the seal. 'So, you've found it. May I see it?' I snatched my hand away and looked at him with such hatred that he pulled back in surprise. His greedy eyes narrowed and he gave a low laugh.

'I see that we understand one another.' He pointed a black gloved finger at me. 'La Paix is mine. Give me the seal. You will be well rewarded.' I shook my head.

Sir Gaston bent close and whispered, 'Don't make me your enemy.' I turned away. 'Then—we are on opposite sides after all, Mariane.'

CHAPTER TWENTY-THREE
SO BE IT!

All night the streets of Orléans were in ferment, with people dancing and singing, praying, feasting. Revellers gathered under our window, keeping us awake with their shouts: '*La Pucelle! Fille de Dieu!* Orléans!'

Whatever Dunois's decision, the people made their opinion clear. They expected Jehanne to attack Les Tourelles. Dunois was forced to bow to their wishes.

The next day Jehanne armed herself for the battle and bade me do the same. I belted my surcoat, sheathed my knife, then reached for the glove, leaving the seal in the box.

'Put on the seal,' Jehanne said. 'Wear it. Sir Gaston will have to kill you to get it, won't he?' We laughed, but inwardly I shivered. 'It won't be today,' Jehanne said, still in good spirits. 'Today will bring a great victory and you will come home safe with your seal.'

God help me, I didn't believe her: I had seen the look in Sir Gaston's eyes and I couldn't afford to fight any private battles out there in the field. So I placed the seal back in the box and put on the glove. I was ready for Les Tourelles.

Once more we rode ahead of the army through the city gate and down to the river. The army massed on the bank, preparing to cross. Behind the ranks of soldiers was a large crowd of citizens. In front of this assembly, Jehanne faced Dunois. He tried one last time to dissuade her.

'We should wait,' he said. 'The English have not retired through weakness. This is a planned strategy. They will have made Les Tourelles practically unassailable, with stockpiles of weapons and supplies. Their finest soldiers will have planned for every form of attack, even cannon. We are ill-advised to move against them without more troops.'

For answer, Jehanne raised her standard and couched it in the cup in her belt. As the white banner unfurled, a great sigh rolled over the assembled company. Pasquerel the priest called out in a ringing voice, 'Let us pray!' Soldiers and citizens dropped to their knees.

Pasquerel waited until, finally, even Dunois bowed his head. During the silence that followed, I expected the priest to lead the ceremony, but it was Jehanne who spoke.

'Dear Lord and Father of all. I pray for the souls of those, our enemy, who shall die at my hands this day. Forgive them their sins and forgive me, and those who follow me, when we fall on our enemy with all the might of Your great purpose. Deliver us from evil thoughts and desires. May our swords strike with honour.' As she finished her prayer, everyone in that company, or so it seemed, uttered a long loud 'Amen!'

The crowd stood up. Jehanne and Dunois now faced them together. Dunois stayed silent.

'This day,' Jehanne cried, 'we shall win Les Tourelles!'

The people at the back of the crowd surged forward. The soldiers in front swayed like wheat in the wind, but

❦ 184 ❦

they held their position. Dunois looked out over them, his people, his soldiers.

'Les Tourelles,' he said. He turned his horse to the boats, then drew his sword and pointed across the river. 'So be it.'

When we reached the bastille, the English were ready and waiting, staring down at us from the top of the earthwork that defended its southern entrance.

A great ditch lay at the foot of the earthwork. Covering themselves with their shields, our men advanced. Those without shields carried ladders and weapons. Moving forward they protected each other. As they entered the ditch, Jehanne and I reined in our chargers to watch. The men were an open target as the enemy hurled down sticks and stones, clods of earth, anything to cause injury. The noise was thunderous. The enemy constantly taunted them with jeers and insults. This clamour, with the continual thud of rocks striking the wooden shields, made my ears ring. But the men kept moving forward.

We were a thousand strong, too many to rout easily. As the next wave swarmed down the bank, Jehanne dismounted, planted her standard at the top of the ditch and called the trumpeters to sound the general assault.

Our advance was relentless. As the last rank of our soldiers put on their shields, the first reached the foot of the earthwork and threw ladders against its walls. Now the English let loose a storm of deadly arrows. Many found their mark and the groans of the victims rent the air. The sound of people in pain can cause panic so, roaring defiance, Jehanne and I now entered the ditch together. The going was harder. We had to climb over our own dead and dying. Gaps opened in our company.

'*Avance*!' cried la Hire, with a great clarion call, throwing his shield aside, risking his life to encourage the men.

'Keep together!' Dunois shouted from his post on top of the ditch.

Time and again we threw ladders up to the earthwork. Time and again they were thrown down into the ditch. The fallen had broken limbs, cracked pates, bloody noses. Too many injuries. At noon, amid English jeers and cat-calls, Jehanne called a halt. 'Retire!' came the shout and the trumpet call. 'Retire!'

We pulled back to Les Augustins, to regroup and tend the wounded. Breathing hard, I sat on the ground outside the fort, resting my head in my hands. The men sat listless, exhausted. Water bearers handed out cups. Cooks set up their trestles with bread and meat. The healers tended the wounded. We ate in a sullen silence. Afterwards, no one moved. A boy took out his pipe and began to play, but was hushed. Were we defeated already?

Then Jehanne appeared, leading her charger.

'Back to it,' she said, grasping the reins, about to mount. When no one moved to her order, she dropped the reins and went to face the men. She stood in front of them and waited.

'There are too many of them,' someone called. 'There must be thousands.'

'There are few compared to us, but our task is greater because they hold the higher ground,' said Jehanne.

'They will never give up!'

'And we cannot be beaten. When the English realize it, they will leave.'

'They fight like demons,' someone said, giving rise to much muttering.

'They are not demons,' Jehanne called. 'They are men and women like us. They eat, sleep, and fight, like us. They feel fear and exhaustion, like us. They think they are stronger, but they are not. This is our country, not theirs.'

Some of the men lifted their heads to look at her. They were listening.

'We bring them a message. God wants them to leave France.' She looked out across the field of faces, now fixed on hers. 'They *will* leave.'

Some of the men hauled themselves to their feet.

'The English don't want to listen, but we shall *make* them listen! To arms. Once more.' She nodded and the rest of the soldiers stood up. As they formed ranks, Jehanne drew her sword and raised it high. 'Brothers-in-arms!' she cried. 'I hoped never to spill any man's blood. But if I have to, I will. I am God's instrument. It is His Desire that we drive back the English. We *shall* drive them back. His Will be done.'

The sea of men swayed as heads lifted to look at the sword.

'God is with us!' she cried. 'We shall not fail.' Crossing themselves the men echoed her words. *'God is with us ... We shall not fail ...'*

'For Orléans ...'

'For Orléans ...'

'For France!'

'For France!'

We gathered our weapons and set off again for Les Tourelles.

CHAPTER TWENTY-FOUR
'YIELD TO THE KING OF HEAVEN!'

'Mariane! Well met!' Didier swarmed up the ladder next to mine. A little way away, Jehanne was climbing the earthwork ahead of us, almost at the top. I saw her turn to draw her axe, which seemed to be caught in her belt. She cried out and fell.

I roared and Didier called, 'What?' then followed my shaking hand as I pointed to Jehanne's body slumped below. She had been hit by an arrow in her left shoulder.

Assailed by a lance thrust at him from above, Didier had to turn back to the fight, but I jumped off the ladder and ran to Jehanne's side. She was still breathing. The soldiers holding the ladder looked at her, dazed, and I knew that if word spread that Jehanne was wounded, the fight might well be over. I picked her up and, supporting her with my shoulder, made angry gestures to tell them to get on with the fight. Jehanne opened her eyes and managed to wave them away. 'It's nothing. Go on, go on.' The men turned back to the battle.

I carried Jehanne to where the porters were placing the wounded and laid her down, where she couldn't be seen. She curled up on her side and hugged her knees. 'It hurts,' she said. 'It hurts.'

I studied the arrow buried deep in her left shoulder. It

must come out or the wound would fester and prove deadly. In spite of her efforts to reassure them, soldiers were leaving the fight to look at her. Jehanne saw them and painfully hoisted herself up into a sitting position. She had her hand pressed to her wound, fingers either side of the bolt.

In a loud voice, to the soldiers, she said, 'Did I not say I should be wounded? This is God's purpose. Go back to the fight. Claim the earthwork, in God's name! Go!' Then she slumped and whispered to me, 'Hide me, Mariane. Don't let them see me like this. Keep me hidden.'

I helped her up and away from the ditch to a more sheltered spot near Les Augustins, where the horses were tethered.

'I must pull out the arrow,' she breathed. 'Give me water.' I pulled off my cap and ran to the bucket of water left for the horses. Then, as I filled it, I heard her cry out. When I got back to her, she had the blood covered arrow in her hand.

I looked at the wound—it must be washed—but the bolt had pierced her armour and left a hole with ragged metal edges pressing into her flesh. There was a deal of blood welling up from it.

Jehanne grabbed the cap, threw some water over her face and drank the rest. 'Help me,' she whispered, trying to unbuckle her breastplate. Horrified, I hesitated, wondering how she would stand the pain of removing it from the wound. 'Make a gag.' She stopped for breath then added, with a faint smile, 'Stop my screams.'

I tore a strip from the hem of my surcoat and twisted

the cloth into a rope, then put it gently round Jehanne's mouth. Fiercely she shook her head until I had pulled it tight, stretching the corners of her mouth back like the grin of a skull. Finally she nodded and I took off the breast-plate.

Afterwards I watched over her while she slept, making sure that no more blood leaked from the wound, which I had bound with more strips of linen. It was deep but not disabling. Sleep was the best remedy.

I bent over her to move her head, which lay awkwardly, to a more comfortable position on the mound of leaves I had put there for a pillow. A shadow passed over us. I looked up into the face of Sir Gaston.

I jumped up and drew my knife, stung to protect Jehanne. Step by step I led him away from her, to the walls of Les Augustins. But she was not his target. I was.

With professional ease, Sir Gaston gripped my right arm with his left hand and pressed me back, round a corner where we would not be seen. His sword, held in his right hand, grazed my cheek, then he moved the tip of it to my throat. I reared and struggled wildly to throw him off, but he increased the pressure on my arm and my knife dropped from my useless fingers.

'I'll take what belongs to me,' he said, and, pressing the tip of his sword into my neck, held out his hand for the seal. With my left hand I reached for my glove, as if to accede to his request but, as my fingers worked to remove it, I saw my chance when his eyes flicked greedily from mine to the glove. A slight distraction, but all I needed. I spun round and kicked hard at the unprotected skirt of his mail. He doubled up, but as I seized my knife and planted myself, ready for the fight, he flicked his sword to catch my blade and knocked it well out of reach.

Then he took my gloved hand, stretched it out and, to my terror, raised his sword to deliver a shearing blow.

Our trumpets sounded. Retreat! Retreat!

'Are we there?' called Jehanne's faint voice.

'Not yet!' someone replied.

Soldiers crowded into view. Some appeared round the corner. They stared at us. Sir Gaston lowered his sword. Then he sheathed it, bowed to me and turned to leave. When the soldiers moved away, he turned back. He seized my hand and roughly pulled off the glove.

'Ah,' he said, 'you're not wearing the seal. Well,' he threw down my hand. 'This isn't finished, *ma chère*.'

Jehanne struggled to stand. 'Where's my sword?' she said. I handed it to her. 'And the standard?' I shook my head. 'Find it, Mariane,' she said.

I walked to where I had a clear view of the earthwork and saw a page pull the standard from where Jehanne had planted it at the edge of the ditch. He passed it to one of the retreating soldiers.

'Can you see it?' Jehanne called. 'What's happening?'

The standard flapped uncertainly as the trumpets sounded again.

'Retreat! Retreat! Always retreat!' Jehanne held her left arm close to her chest. 'Fetch my horse.'

It was no use disputing with her. I got the horse and

she mounted it, then swung it round until she had sighted the standard. Pricking her horse's sides, she set off at a brisk pace.

She seized the standard from the retreating soldier and pointed it toward Les Tourelles. The army, stretched out from there to Les Augustins, was in retreat. Now the men came to a halt where they stood and awaited Jehanne's orders.

'*Avance!*' she cried. '*Avance! Avance au Nom de Dieu!*'

Like a force come fresh to the fight, they turned again to renew their assault on the earthwork.

I ran back to my position and saw Didier on a ladder ahead of me. As our troops pressed forward again, Jehanne followed and doggedly scaled the earthwork. The hours of struggle had taken their toll on the English as well as the French and the hail of missiles had dwindled. The fighting was now hand to hand.

Jehanne found a firm footing and stood at the top of the earthwork, silhouetted against the blue sky. As if untouched by the battle around her, she again raised her sword, this time reversing it and holding it by the blade, so that it became a cross for all to see, French and English. Her voice rang out across the battle field: 'Yield! Yield to the King of Heaven. He will have mercy on your immortal souls.'

From the top of the earthwork I saw everything. The English were throwing down their weapons and pouring back across the drawbridge over the Loire. But brave Orléans citizens had bypassed our fight and carried out their own, running a great barge full of stinking rubbish under the drawbridge then setting fire to it. As the retreating English forces attempted to cross, the bridge collapsed beneath them. All on the bridge were drowned, including, as Jehanne had foreseen, the commander, Glasdale.

At this catastrophe, the rest of the English, within the bastille and without, surrendered. We took nearly two hundred prisoners.

Les Tourelles was ours.

When we returned to Orléans, the news had preceded us: the Orléannais danced in the streets. With a cloak over her armour, Jehanne went straight to the cathedral, but I hurried to our lodging, driven by an increasing fear.

My fear was well founded. When I took the box from my pack and looked inside, I found my missal untouched, but the seal had gone.

CHAPTER TWENTY-FIVE
ST LAURENT

S ir Gaston. He had stolen my seal. Like someone brain-sick, I searched the crowded streets for him, elbowing my way through the shoals of revellers, forever imagining that I could see the corner of his black cloak disappearing ahead of me, just out of reach, around every corner. With each stride my conviction grew: it had to be him. No one else had seen the seal, only he and Jehanne.

'Mariane!' Didier crashed into me, knocking me off balance, then clumsily set me straight again, his face alight with joy; he was merry with drink. In each hand he carried a pig's bladder on a stick. He tapped me playfully on the head with them. 'I crown thee king—of fools!' he shrieked.

I pushed him away.

'"*Le cochon, il t'embrasse—*"' he sang, aiming the bladder at me again.

'"*—elle fuit de son baiser!*"' someone pointed out, as his friends crowded round us, laughing and singing, their faces sweaty, like satyrs', in the light of their torches.

'We're taking a dip in the Loire! Come and join us. Look—Matthieu can't wait!' In spite of the long walk to the river, one of the squires hurled away his shirt and pulled down his trousers.

Didier took my arm, steering me away. 'We'll see yer later,' he called. 'Save us some of that wine.'

As the squires roared down to the river, Didier propelled me into the shadow of a deserted alley. 'What is it?' he said, suddenly sober.

I stared back at him. Could I trust him?

'What's wrong?' he said. 'Mariane?' He touched my shoulder.

I wrenched myself away and walked deeper into the shadows. Didier followed. 'It's all right. I know all about yer. I know who you are. You're Mariane de Courcey, daughter of François de Louvier, heir to La Paix. It's all right. I'm on your side.'

I swung round and jutted my chin. Didier looked at me closely, then said, 'So, 'e's got the seal?'

I nodded.

'Ah. I wondered why 'e left in such a 'urry, in his spy-master's guise. 'e's probably gone to La Paix.'

I marched past him and out of the alley. Didier caught me as I turned into the main street. 'Where yer going?'

I snatched his little finger and locked it with mine. He worked out the meaning of the sign. 'Pax? Ah, La Paix.'

I left him and walked on, heading for my lodging where I would take leave of Jehanne, then saddle up for the long journey.

'You can't go alone! Do you even know the way?' Didier dogged my steps. 'Huh. I was going to Paris in the mornin'! I was going to start a new life in Paris! My friends are expectin' me.'

I walked on.

'Eh, what's the big 'urry? I doubt Sir Gaston'll get there before yer, even if yer leave it for a day or two.'

I stopped and looked at him, questioningly.

'I fouled his watersack, so 'e won't get far. With any luck, by this time tomorrow 'e'll be 'oled up in some tavern, struggling to hang on to 'is wormy guts.'

I smothered a giggle.

'When 'e left in such a 'urry, I saw my chance. 'e told me I was to wait 'ere, but I made my own plans. Tomorrow at dawn, I was out of 'ere, 'eading for Paris. Didn't want him catching up with me and hauling me back for a beating, so I laced his water with a strong dose of rhubarb.'

I barked with laughter and hugged Didier. Then I stood back and solemnly stared at him.

Straight away Didier said, 'Yes, aw'right. La Paix: I'm coming with yer.'

As we shook hands to seal the bargain, trumpets sounded a midnight curfew over the town. 'Meet me 'ere at dawn,' he said.

Jehanne was cleaning her armour when I walked into the lodging, and when she looked up at me, I froze with a forewarning, shivering at what she was about to say. 'The English have gathered at St Laurent. We must fight again for Orléans, in the morning.'

Angily I roared. Surely she had done enough? But Jehanne patiently explained, 'The English are dogged fighters. They will never give in, to the last man; they will never surrender. They are abandoning all other positions, but not St Laurent. It's their final hold on Orléans and they will make us fight for it. If we breach the bastille there, they will give up the city. St Laurent is where they will make their last stand.'

She went on wiping mud from the greave which she had wedged between her knee and the table top, so taking the strain from her painful shoulder.

I went to help, but she shook her head.

'A soldier must keep her own gear in trim,' she said, smiling. 'Now sit with me and tell me what's wrong.'

I had only to show her the place on my finger where I had worn the seal.

'He has taken it, then. I thought he would if he had an opportunity: there was such greed in his eyes. And now you want to fight him for it. He has gone to La Paix?'

I nodded.

'So, you're leaving.'

Torn by conflicting loyalties, I bowed my head. *Not if you need me*.

'Orléans is only the beginning, Mariane,' she said, quietly, going on with her polishing. 'What about Paris? The English still hold it and all the cities between. What about Auxerre and Troyes? God has told me to crown the king, so I must head for Reims, fighting through every city on the way.' She sighed. 'So many battles.'

Startled by the note of weariness in her voice, I looked up at her.

'But God is with us: we are all in His hands.' Jehanne was smiling again. 'Get some rest and ask God what to do. You will have your answer by morning.'

That night I slept fitfully, riven by dreams of La Paix and St Laurent, Paris, Reims, and a France lost again to the English.

I woke to the clatter of horses' hooves on the cobbles and the jingle of harness. Jehanne knelt in prayer and, remembering that it was Sunday, the Lord's Day, I knelt by her side.

Arming herself, Jehanne put on a coat of light mail: her breast plate would have been too painful to wear on top of her wound. I put on my leather jerkin and surcoat, took my knife, a small axe and a shield, then followed her downstairs and into the stable yard to mount our horses. It was not yet dawn. I would meet Didier on the way and hope that he understood my decision.

As we rode along the main street, Didier caught up with us and rode at my side. We exchanged a look. He was armed for the coming battle just as I was; on hearing about St Laurent, he had also decided to stay for the fight.

'Sir Gaston will have to wait. In great discomfort, I hope,' he chuckled.

As we made our way out of the city more and more troops joined the company. We were a mass of chevaliers, of foot soldiers and townspeople who marched with whatever weapons they could find: pitchforks and shovels, staffs, and stones. There were even children carrying bunches of stinging nettles and thorny branches, all singing as they went.

We arrived at the field in front of the bastille just after dawn, the rising sun glinting gold stars from our armour. We drew a halt just out of bowshot. St Laurent was eerily quiet.

'Where are they?' Didier whispered, echoing the question repeated throughout the ranks.

'The goddams have skipped it!' someone said. Low laughter greeted the comment.

Jehanne, in the middle of the front line holding her standard, held up her hand for silence.

From either side of the bastille the English came out to meet us, silently forming their battle lines with precision. The archers came first, taking up their positions behind pointed stakes, which I now realized they had already hammered into the ground in a long line, three or four deep, angled to cause grievous harm to our charging cavalry.

Between them stood men-at-arms, on foot, bearing sword and pole-axe. Behind them more of the same. Their captains, the knights on horseback, stood ready on the flanks; once in position, they were all as still as stone.

An English commander raised his arm and the archers strung their bows and pulled them taut. A cold tremor passed through me. *Agincourt*. This was the same English challenge to our spirited cavalry. The English would wait for us to make the first move. Impatient with the waiting game, our chevaliers would mount a glorious charge. Honour demanded it. But at the same instant, the English longbowmen would loose such a storm of arrows that the sky would be black with them. Like my father, our brave chevaliers would die.

As Jehanne raised the standard, I grabbed her arm, shaking my head. Around us the knights grew restive, the destriers stamping their hooves and circling with frustration. They could smell the fight. Why could they not charge?

The archers opposite were as still as painted effigies, watching us with deadly focus, each man's eye on his target. No arrow wasted. *Agincourt*.

Jehanne put her hand over mine, then let go and began to walk her horse towards the enemy lines.

'Today is the Lord's day,' she said, looking out over their assembled company. 'Almighty God shall decide the issue. Make no mistake, we shall engage our enemy. But first we shall pray.'

At her signal four priests, dressed in their Sunday vestments, emerged from the ranks and set down a table, on which one of them placed a large gold cross. Jehanne dismounted and, handing her standard to a page, knelt at the altar with her back to the English lines. She stretched her arms wide and threw back her head, then, in a ringing voice, she called out, 'Our Father, Which art in Heaven—'

I dismounted and knelt with her and so did Didier, one either side, and all our French soldiers, heads bowed, some helmets in hand, added their voices.

The priest completed our devotions. '*In nomine patris*—'

Jehanne, still kneeling, now bowed her head and clasped her hands in front of her.

Something made me look at the English lines. I waited to make certain of what I was seeing, then touched her arm to make her look too. The English were lowering their weapons. Line by line, they were turning away. They were leaving the field.

'The day is ours,' she said, getting to her feet. The English force was heading away from the Bastille. Jehanne mounted her horse and watched them, then she swung round to face her army. 'This day is truly ours!' she called. 'Thanks be to God!'

The men cheered and threw their helmets in the air. Finally Orléans was free.

CHAPTER TWENTY-SIX
LA PAIX

D idier and I left the following dawn, after an unhappy farewell to Jehanne. At the start her mission had seemed clear: to raise the siege of Orléans, then crown the dauphin. Now the first part was done and the English were in complete disarray, I thought the second part would follow in good order. My thoughts were so unclouded, so innocent. How little I understood.

But Jehanne knew that Orléans was only the beginning. The enemy had been weakened but not finally defeated.

'I must crown the dauphin in Reims,' she said. She sighed and moved to the window to look up into the clean blue sky. 'If God wills that we reach the cathedral.' She turned back to us. 'There are so many towns still in English hands, between here and Reims. But I *have* to get there.' She banged her clenched fist on the wall. 'A French king will unite all of France,' she said. 'I must crown the dauphin. Then the English will leave.'

Her eyes focused on me and Didier. 'But you came to tell me something, Mariane.'

'It's like this—er—Je'anne,' Didier said. 'Mariane is keen to go after Sir Gaston—'

'—who has her seal.'

'Yes. And I've said I'll go wiv her. We'll ride together to

the dispute and Mariane, Sir François's rightful heir, will make herself known at La Paix.'

'God thrive your venture, my cousin,' she said. 'I shall pray for you and I shall miss you. Hurry back.'

At that, tearful, I hugged her close.

'Send word if you need us,' said Didier.

Jehanne let me go and said, 'I'll ask Pasquerel to send our news to La Paix. Before long, God willing, I shall be in Reims and then afterwards, who knows? When the last enemy has left France, perhaps we shall meet again in Domrémy, when we go back to be farm girls.' Jehanne and I both wept then. It seemed such a remote thing; impossible, like wishing to be a child again.

As we left, I tried to think only of my intention: to dispute with Sir Gaston for the inheritance of La Paix and to exact vengeance for the murder of my mother. When I had settled that score I would fly back to Jehanne. The venture was simple enough in its outline, but the details alarmed and overwhelmed me if I tried to secure them, so, pushing my fears away, and trusting to destiny, I rode out with Didier, north from Orléans.

La Paix appeared in front of us, just as Didier had described it. A golden haze on the horizon, firming with every mile into the outline of a golden castle. Sandstone, battlemented, easy to defend, built high on top of a steep hill, and sur-rounded by a moat of still clear water. Green watercress growing from its sides in fat cushions.

We rode over a wide drawbridge and were heartily wel-comed inside by an old and faithful retainer, Laurent. We learned that Sir Gaston had not yet arrived and shared a grin. Didier's foul-water plan must have worked.

'We'll go straight to the priory,' said Didier, leading the way as the gates swung shut behind us. 'That's where my lady is, Ghislaine, sister to Sir Gaston and your father.'

We dismounted, tied up the horses, then walked into the herb garden at the front of the long low priory building. 'Didier!' The lady Ghislaine put down the herbs she was cutting and came across, smiling at Didier as if he were a long lost son. Then, she gave him a questioning look. 'Don't worry, milady, there's just the two of us. Sir Gaston intended to come, but 'as been delayed.' Didier grinned, then stood aside to introduce me to my aunt.

She gasped and clapped a hand to her mouth. 'Eloise!' she breathed. Didier nodded. 'My lady, this is your niece, Mariane de Courcey.'

'You're the copy of your mother,' she said and tears glistened in her eyes. 'Welcome. Welcome to La Paix. Welcome home, *ma fille*,' she said.

She gave us both an arm, hugging us to her sides as she walked us inside the priory. 'Come, come—oh, come and tell me everything.'

Within the hour, Didier had told her my story and explained the loss of my voice. Lady Ghislaine had listened, hardly able to take her eyes from me as I tucked into the bread and cheese she had laid out for us. She poured me wine and I drank deep.

'The seal. So he has it,' she said at last. 'Well, we must seek the advice of a lawyer and the man we need is in

Troyes; Signor Fabri, an old friend of my father. Didier, you must fetch him.'

Didier bowed his head. 'I'll leave straightaway, *ma dame*,' he said.

Lady Ghislaine looked at him and said, 'No. A few more hours won't make any difference; you need a good night's rest. It's a very long ride. You can leave first thing in the morning.'

That evening, while Didier renewed old acquaintances in the wine cellar, I sat with my aunt as she told me all she could about my father and showed me some of his things. She had his shield and some of his weapons and trophies of war: an English sword and war saddle. I already knew that he was a hardy soldier and a skilled swordsman, but I learned he had a scholarly side too. There were books, copied and decorated by the craftsmen at the priory: St Mark's Gospel, the Psalms, and the Lives of the Saints.

'He was a Christian knight,' said my aunt Ghislaine. 'And for his sake, my home will always be yours, whatever the outcome of your dispute with Gaston.'

Laurent tapped on my door the next morning and brought in an armful of clothes. 'A gift from my lady,' he said.

I picked over the clothes. Women's clothes. It seemed an age ago that I had last worn women's dress and I had never worn anything as fine as these. I chose a blue woollen gown with long sleeves and cream embroidery at neck and hem. It felt strange when I put it on, as if I were changing myself into someone else. Running my fingers through my short hair, I wondered if I would ever see myself as the lady of the manor at La Paix.

I thought Didier would laugh when he saw me but he seemed shocked. His face coloured and he said not a word, but mounted his horse and rode off on his mission to Troyes. At the gate, though, he did turn to look back at me, just once, then he rode off as if devils from hell were after him.

While we waited for Didier's return, my aunt Ghislaine and I settled down together in the blessed refuge of La Paix. Those were golden summer days, when I rose at dawn, startled at first to find myself away from the battle-field, then with relief as I got up and took a leisurely walk through the soft liquid air of the gardens.

The manor itself, grand and imposing, was unoccupied; its tapestries stored in chests; its treasures locked away; its staff of servants reduced by war. I wandered through the rooms imagining what life had been like there when my father had been alive, remembering old troubadour songs and picking up a pinch of my fine gown to dance a few steps in the empty solar.

The priory, where my aunt had rooms, had remained unchanged from my father's day, with the same dozen monks and, in the infirmary, two serving-girls and old Laurent, to assist my aunt in looking after the patients, all folk from the surrounding towns and villages, who looked on La Paix for their protection, and to its owner as their liege lord to whom they would, in return, give their free service, in peacetime or war.

I put a sacking apron over my fine woollen gown and walked along the row of beds. Fever, colick, wounds, St Anthony's fire, these were all ailments I recognized and had remedies for. This was a task to keep me busy while I was waiting, so each day I took my turn in tending the sick, as I used to at grandmère's side, at home in Reims.

But every day after my duties, I went to stand for a while on the drawbridge to scan the long road that led to Troyes, watching for any sign of Didier's return. Like a worm in the pit of my stomach writhed the fear that Sir Gaston would come before Didier had returned. With that in mind, every day too I found time to change back into my shirt and trousers and do battle practice with a quarterstaff on the ground behind the manor, where weeds had grown over the lists.

Didier had been gone over a month when a messenger came with bad news. Didier had found Signor Fabri, but on the way out of Troyes they had been accosted by an armed company, acting under Sir Gaston's orders, and although the lawyer had escaped unrecognized, Didier had been hauled back into Sir Gaston's service. The battle for Jargeau—a town held by the English that lay between Orléans and Reims—was at hand and all men were needed.

'Didier won't come to any harm, Mariane,' my aunt assured me. 'He's much too useful to Gaston. Don't worry. And Signor Fabri will come to La Paix. I know he will.'

The messenger brought good news too, a letter from Jehanne. '*Jhesus Maria,*' it began. '*To my cousin Mariane, the blessing of God and His angels. We have met with success in every battle. Now the way is clear to Reims and the holy coronation. God grant that we reach there soon. Pray for me. Jehanne.'*

It was two more weeks before Signor Fabri arrived. I had returned from battle practice and, hot from my exertions, stood in my shift at the window of my room looking down into the courtyard. I had closed my eyes, but opened them again at the sudden creak of the drawbridge. The hooves of two horses clattered on the cobbles, but before I could make out the faces of the riders, they had passed out of sight. I flung on a green linen gown and ran downstairs to my aunt's room, just in time to see the guests arrive.

Didier? No.

'Signor Fabri, welcome, welcome to La Paix,' said my aunt, as I followed the visitors—an old man and his servant—into the room.

'*Grazia*, Ghislaine,' said the old man, seating himself in the best chair, next to the basket of sweet-smelling herbs which he gently rubbed in his fingers. He signalled his manservant to leave.

'Laurent?' With a graceful gesture my aunt gave orders for refreshments and quarters to be found for the man, then she called to me, hovering on the threshold. 'Mariane!'

Stumbling into the room, I managed to remember my manners and make a half-decent courtesy to our honoured guest.

'So, this is a dispute of inheritance,' Signor Fabri began in his thick Italian accent and, accepting a cup of wine from my aunt, he settled himself to listen to her story of my father's legacy and his final wish that La Paix go to

Eloise de Courcey, the wife of his heart, and after her, to their child. To me.

'There is a will?' said the lawyer. My aunt shook her head.

'I have never seen one. When François died—ah, it was a time of madness, signor—we were in hiding, never knowing whether the English would come and claim him for ransom, dead or alive. There was barely time to say a prayer. But my brother told me his wishes, for Eloise de Courcey to inherit the estate and, after her, their child Mariane, here. We managed to send her mother some things which, Eloise having died—God rest her soul—have come to Mariane. He sent Eloise the seal, the de Louvier seal, and Mariane inherited it, on her mother's death. She kept it hidden, but my brother Gaston has stolen it, so that he can claim La Paix for his own. Without a will, it is all he needs.'

Signor Fabri looked at me like a hawk, with his piercing dark eyes.

'You have proof of this? You call your uncle a thief? It is a most serious charge.'

A thief and a violent bully, I thought, looking at the worn lines on my aunt's face. *She took twenty strokes and never uttered a sound.*

'Mariane,' Signor Fabri called for my attention. 'You have proof that Sir Gaston took the seal?'

I shook my head.

'Well, well.' Signor Fabri sat back and sipped his wine.

I flashed an angry glance at my aunt. This whole thing was a waste of time. Proof. I needed proof. Without it Signor Fabri would not believe me.

'I should like to see what remains,' he said. 'The box and its contents.'

At my aunt's request I fetched my box.

'Ah. A soldier's glove.' Signor Fabri carefully took out my father's glove. 'It 'as been cleaned and worn since you received it?' I nodded and mentally kicked myself. 'Marked here, possibly, with the imprint of a seal,' he murmured, passing the tip of his little finger over the leather.

Possibly? It was there.

'And a soldier's badge,' he said, stretching the soiled linen between his fingers. 'Without doubt the de Louvier emblem, two blue chevrons on a white roundel. Evidently torn from some soldier's coat.'

My father's coat! I looked at my aunt, but she merely raised her hand and shook her head with a slight gesture, as if to say I must be patient.

'You packed the box?'

'I did, signor,' she said, 'on my brother's instructions.'

'And he gave you the de Louvier seal to send to Eloise?'

'He did. I wrapped it in the badge he tore from his tunic.'

'So, he made clear his wishes. And you claim that Gaston has taken it back? Hush—' Signor Fabri quelled my aunt's protest. '—I mean no disrespect, Ghislaine, but we must look at this with a most acute legal eye. Proof is required, if Mariane's claim has any chance at all of succeeding.'

Signor Fabri took up the missal. 'Well, leave the seal aside for the time being. Mm. A missal. Expensively bound.' He opened the cover to the frontispiece. 'Marked with a name: *François Etienne de Louvier, Chevalier du Roi de France. Luca in servitio Deo fecit.* Mm. It would seem to be genuine.'

Of course it's genuine! At my growl of frustration, Signor

Fabri paused to stare at me until I dropped my gaze, then he leafed idly through the pages of the prayer book, before closing it and placing it on the table before him.

'Very well. These are poignant souvenirs of a fine soldier. You must value them highly, signorina.' Narrowing my eyes, I returned his stare.

'So you believe us?' said my aunt.

'Though I have been at some distance from La Paix, since your father died I have watched over you all. It was easy to see which way the wind blew when François brought Eloise to La Paix. Loving her he made an enemy of his brother, and envy and avarice worked their harm on Gaston. In my view, François would certainly have cut his brother out of the inheritance and it does not surprise me to hear that he wanted it to go to Eloise.

'But my opinion weighs nothing against the weight of your uncle's claim, if, as you say, he has the de Louvier seal.' Signor Fabri snapped shut the lid of the box. 'François made no will, you say? That surprises me. I must call on the prior.'

Signor Fabri fixed me with his eyes again. 'May I take away your box and its contents, signorina, for further close examination?'

I nodded briskly. Signor Fabri stood up and tucked the box under his arm. There must have been a shine of hope on my face, because as he came round from the other side of the table, he said gravely, 'Mariane, Mariane. I have to tell you that without a will and without the seal, your claim is hopeless.'

I bit my lip and turned away so that neither of them would see the angry tears in my eyes.

CHAPTER TWENTY-SEVEN
NEWS FROM REIMS

June ended with the hay harvest; July opened with storms. We saved most of the herbs, essential medicines, but lost several acres of wheat, flattened by freakish hail. Some said this meant God was angry for some reason, but I remembered grandmère's advice never to blame God for bad weather and, since it was bound to happen, to lay up plenty of stores against it. I was pleased that my aunt Ghislaine followed this advice too, making use of her stock of dried herbs where the fresh were too battered, and bartering her remedies with her neighbours for supplies of wheat flour.

God forgive me, far away from the battlefield, untouched by the threat of war, I sank every day deeper and deeper into my new way of life at the priory. It was a well of healing from which I drank deeply, and my aunt wholly embraced me as her own. Then, step by step, as I proved myself, she became less of a mother to me and more of a friend. Side by side we stayed all day in the infirmary until, as weeks passed, we began to work in full sympathy, without the need for words, each moving to help the other where required, each stepping in to take up the slack from the other's weary hands.

There was still no sign of Sir Gaston. But, towards the end of the month, there came another letter from Jehanne.

After vespers one evening, my aunt and I sat in the garden, as was our custom at day's end, at the foot of the western wall, on a low stone bench set in a bank of thyme and camomile. We rested our heads and shoulders against the warm stone and listened to the hum of the bees. It was our quiet time. Jehanne's letter had come earlier by messenger. I had read it through quickly, as soon as I could, but now I asked my aunt to read it aloud to me.

Jhesus Maria. To my cousin, Mariane, the blessing of God and His angels and to her aunt, Ghislaine de Louvier, greetings.

Much has happened since I last sent word, but be assured that all is well. Mariane, I have all but accomplished my mission, all that I set out to do. I write from Reims and by the time this letter reaches you, the king will have been crowned. We shall have a French king at last, and so prove the fire of our spirit to the English. God be praised.

But I run ahead of myself. We still have to secure the allegiance of the Duke of Burgundy and force him to abandon the English side. I can hardly bring myself to write his name, but I must look truth in the eye and I must not waver. Many are still of the Burgundian party and support the English cause. After the coronation I shall write to Burgundy, demanding his loyalty to God and to France.

On the way here we were called to battle at Auxerre, where the gates were shut against us. The town turned its back on the dauphin, and la Tremouille—I wish he were not such a favourite with the dauphin—la Tremouille took a bribe of money to lead us away and leave it in peace. They are Burgundians all, but, at the dauphin's behest, that is what we did. So, that city still watches us from the shadows, as if we were still at war. No good will come of it.

The same thing would have happened at Troyes, which also closed its gates at first, but fortunately we met friends there, and we were eventually welcomed into the city. It isn't the townspeople who fear us and turn away, but their leaders. They all wait to see who is the stronger: English or French, then they will change flags accordingly. Our brave people are led by donkeys, or reeds that bend with the wind.

'Good news: the road to Reims led through Chalons, and there I met many old friends from home who had travelled to join us. They brought news of my parents. My mother prays for me every day in the church, and my father goes with her. He has forgiven me, Mariane. Tears spring to my eyes to think of it. And he has come to Reims with Durand—Durand! How long ago and far away it seems when we left Domrémy that night. They will be at the cathedral and afterwards we shall all meet again.

The dauphin goes to the cathedral soon to spend the night hours in vigil. It's very close now, so very close. I have done my best. I have gambled the utmost. To God be the rest.

Pray for me.

Jehanne.

That night I hardly slept for the excitement of Jehanne's news. By now it would be over. She had fulfilled her mission: France would have a king.

'Mariane!' My aunt Ghislaine cried out, an urgent call. 'Mariane!' It was dawn.

I pulled on my gown and ran barefoot downstairs, tying my belt as I went.

'Mariane, look!' As my aunt moved away from the doorway into the solar, I saw someone standing behind her with a cup of wine in his hand. *Didier*. With a cry, I rushed at him and hugged his breath away, and his wine cup fell to the floor. The noise brought me to my senses and I stood back from him, my face burning with confusion.

'So, you're pleased to see me then?' he said, then we both laughed and my confusion faded away like mist in the sun.

'I'll fetch some breakfast,' said my aunt, leaving us alone together.

'You look different,' Didier said.

I shrugged as if I didn't care what I looked like and motioned him to a seat. We sat on stools at opposite sides of the fireplace. I pointed at him.

'Oh, fanks, I've been better. Sir Gaston was furious with me for leaving 'im and me back still bears the scars.'

Shocked, I stood up. So did Didier. 'It's . . . er . . . it's nuffink,' he said. 'Sit down, do. It's just that when it rains, I can—it feels—' We both sat down again.

After telling me all the news of Jehanne and the continuing battles and how many people were answering her call, Didier said, 'Sir Gaston's coming 'ere today. Sent me ahead with 'is orders. I'm to make sure that the manor house is ready for his occupation and there are a few particklers to take care of too.' He counted off the list on his fingers. 'Side of roast venison. Barrel of claret. Feather bolster. Two eggs and a fresh loaf every morning. E'll be here by nightfall.'

Again I jumped up, as my aunt appeared with a tray of bread, roast pork, stewed apple and rosehip. 'What is it?' she said.

Didier looked at the food and licked his bottom lip. 'Now that's a sight for sore eyes,' he said.

CHAPTER TWENTY-EIGHT
MY CLAIM IS HEARD

I had just finished sweeping the floor of the infirmary when Didier looked in to say that Sir Gaston was approaching La Paix with a party of men-at-arms and he must go down to see to the horses. The news made my hands tremble, but I forced myself to set my broom carefully aside and untie my apron. I took deep breaths and readied myself to meet my enemy, to confront him in the dispute for La Paix. These past weeks had made the estate and its inhabitants part of me, planting a new way of life in my heart. La Paix was my home and I would not give it up without a fight.

Sir Gaston pushed his way through those gathered in courteous welcome: my aunt and me, Brother Martin and Brother Denis, healers from the priory, all standing at the gate. Brushing aside my aunt's courtesies, Sir Gaston looked up at the derelict manor and said, 'Is the house not ready? Did you not receive my instructions?' Without waiting for a reply, he strode up to the main entrance and pushed at the door. Rainwater had swelled the wood and he had to shove hard with his shoulder to open it a mere hand's-breadth.

'You will be more comfortable in the priory, brother,' called my aunt, as Sir Gaston forced the door open at last, causing the wood to crack and splinter, and went inside.

Rage flared up in my breast: he was behaving as if he were lord of the manor already and there was no respect or reverence in his actions. He had no feeling for La Paix, except as a symbol of wealth and power and his presence here was a stain on my father's memory. I must stop him. I went forward, but my aunt touched my arm to prevent me.

Sir Gaston emerged from the house. 'DIDIER!' he roared, stalking towards the stables. My aunt stepped into his path.

'I told Didier not to prepare the manor. We now live in the priory, until the rightful heir is declared.'

Again Sir Gaston pushed past her. 'I am lord of La Paix,' he said, in a low dangerous voice. 'Be so good, sister, as to prepare rooms for me.' Sir Gaston raised his voice and shouted back at her, as he strode down towards the stables, 'In the manor house.'

My aunt raised her voice to match his. 'Here is Mariane de Courcey, brother.'

Sir Gaston stopped walking, then swung round, his face dark as thunder.

'She will dispute your right to give orders here.'

Sir Gaston came back to us and, staring deep into my eyes, said, 'Get my rooms ready yourself, Ghislaine. Now!'

'I will not.'

The walls echoed the crack as the flat of his gloved hand hit my aunt's face, swiping her away like an annoying insect. She fell awkwardly to the ground and lay still. By instinct, I sprang at my uncle like a novice, using fists and feet to strike, and was thrown down for my pains, at my aunt's side, my head throbbing from a hard blow. I scrambled to my knees and looked up at my uncle, as murder opened its eyes in my heart.

Sir Gaston looked down at me and laughed, then took off his right glove to reveal the de Louvier seal, twisting it so that the gold flashed in the sunlight.

'There will be no dispute,' he said, and his voice, a cold whisper, was like vitriol dripping on to metal.

'Gaston! My boy! We should nevertheless examine your niece's claim.' Signor Fabri's voice called out, calmly and steadily, as he emerged from the herb garden, supported on the arm of Laurent. 'Gaston! Well met, well met. How are you? What news?' he continued in the same unhurried tones, while moving forward with great care, as if approaching a madman or a rabid dog that might any moment flash out into savagery. As he passed by, he gestured sharply to me with stabbing fingers behind his back, to take myself and my aunt from the scene.

I put my arm under my aunt's shoulder and helped her to her feet, watching with amazement as Sir Gaston bowed to Signor Fabri, like a son with a well-loved father, allowing himself to be led away. As they disappeared, Laurent hurried to help me take my aunt into the infirmary.

That night we dined as friends and family, burying our differences. No one mentioned my aunt's bruised cheek and she presided over the table as if Sir Gaston were the prodigal son just returned, producing a fine feast of fresh bread, curd cheese, baked fowl, and pike. Was this why he finally agreed to live with us in the priory, pending a hearing of my claim, mellowed into it on a full stomach?

Without seeming to, I paid careful attention to his conversation with Signor Fabri and discovered the true explanation. Signor Fabri, his father's good friend, was, I quickly saw, an excellent advocate who knew how to use persuasive arguments to win his point. He spoke to Sir Gaston in clear reasonable terms, reminding him that as master of La Paix, liege lord of the demesne, he was the very symbol of law for the region, and should therefore establish his ownership within the law, by exemplary legal means, so that there could be no further dispute.

They were fine persuasive words, but I could see signs of the discomfort they wrought in Sir Gaston—in his hooded eyes and furrowed brow, in his tapping fingers. How he longed to march into La Paix at the head of a well-armed company and take it by force, cutting a way through this lawyers' talk with the keen edge of his sword.

I recognized the signs because I had them too. I could not sit still and I couldn't eat. With balled fists hidden in my lap, I studied his face and burned to smash him to destruction, and so find my way to heart's ease.

But both he and I were forced to endure the ritual of the meal and the course of law, as proposed by Signor Fabri.

The next morning my aunt had the refectory tables moved out of the hall and two rows of chairs set out, facing each other, on opposite sides of the hearth. She and I sat on one side. Sir Gaston on the other. He had dispensed with his men-at-arms, sending them away to find hospitality in the village, but called Didier to stand behind him.

With his back to the fire, at the head of the room, Signor Fabri sat at a small table, which I recognized as my aunt's sewing table brought from the solar. Now it served as a judge's desk. I was on Signor Fabri's left, Sir Gaston on his right. I looked in despair at my aunt. There were so few of us that it didn't seem a proper court.

Soon, though, I noticed that a crowd of people were silently filing in, taking up places along each wall at the back of the hall. Some I recognized from the estate: cooks and gardeners, the miller and his family, the blacksmith, the carpenter. Some I had helped to treat in the infirmary, my patients, now recovered. I nodded and smiled, acknowledging their greetings.

More and more people filed in. I had not realized how many lives might be affected by this day's proceedings. The number doubled and trebled, and still more filed in, all folk dependent on the estate at La Paix and the power of those who ruled here. They had come to witness as judgement was given.

Wherever I looked their faces comforted me. They could not have made it more plain whom they preferred as their liege-master. My stomach turned as I began to realize what this hearing meant, that my future and theirs hung on the decision made at the end of the hearing by Signor Fabri. Mine was flimsy evidence. It lay on the table in front of him, the contents of my box: the glove, the badge, and the missal. Without the will, without my father's seal, it wasn't enough.

Once the room was full, Sir Gaston, lounging in his chair, said, 'Let's get on with it.'

With a sharp glance in his direction, Signor Fabri said quietly, 'The law takes its own time, Sir Gaston, and will not be hurried.' Gesturing to the three of us, he said, 'Now will you all stand.' We stood up and faced him.

Addressing Sir Gaston, he said, 'Milord Gaston Guilbert de Louvier, Chevalier de France, do you swear in the name of Almighty God to tell the whole truth and nothing but the truth?'

Sir Gaston gave a desultory nod.

'Will you give your response out loud, so that all may hear?'

Sir Gaston retorted, 'For God's sake—'

'Milord de Louvier—' Signor Fabri's voice was sharp as a blade and produced a response.

'Very well. I swear.'

'Thank you, milord,' said Signor Fabri with exaggerated courtesy.

'And you, Mariane Eloise de Courcey, do you swear in the name of Almighty God, and on your immortal soul, to tell the truth and nothing but the truth?'

Fervently, I nodded.

'Who speaks for you?'

I touched my aunt's arm. 'I do, she said.

Signor Fabri took my aunt's oath.

'Milord,' he said, addressing Sir Gaston, 'it is correct that you claim title to the manor house, the lands, and all that pertains to the estate of La Paix, formerly the property of your brother, François de Louvier, Chevalier de France?'

'La Paix is mine. I have the seal.'

Sir Gaston held up his right hand for all to see.

'May I see it?' said Signor Fabri. Sir Gaston took off the ring and handed it to him and he examined it for a few moments before holding it out for my aunt to examine. 'Ghislaine de Louvier, is this the de Louvier seal?'

'It is,' my aunt said solemnly. Signor Fabri took back the seal and closed his fist over it.

'Then I claim it as evidence while this hearing is in session.'

'What—?' Gaston protested.

Signor Fabri held up one finger as a warning before laying the seal on the table next to the glove. 'For the time being,' he said, 'the seal belongs to the court.' Then he spoke to my aunt.

'Ghislaine de Louvier, will you now relate for those present the story of your brother François's death and, as far as you know them and swear them to be, his final wishes with regard to the estate of La Paix?'

'I will,' my aunt replied, and then she told again how my father had been mortally wounded at Agincourt and had been brought home to die at La Paix, and she told of my father's love for my mother, of how he had brought her from Reims to live here, and how difficult it had been for her to become the lady of the manor.

'You see, Eloise convinced herself that it was wrong for her to live at La Paix. She was ashamed not to have brought any wealth to the estate. Nothing could shake her of the conviction that she was living above her station. And there were those who made sure she was reminded of it.' Here, she paused to stare at Sir Gaston.

'Life was made unbearable for her whenever Sir François was away. And as the war took him away more and more often, she began to long to go back to Reims. Finally, knowing that she carried François's child, she left La Paix and returned to her childhood home. But we remained good friends, exchanging news, by means of letters, as often as we could.

'When, within months of her leaving, François was fatally wounded, I immediately sent for her. But the child was almost ready to be born and she was unable to make the long journey. On François's instructions, given to me as he lay dying, I packed the box—' She pointed to the box on the table in front of Signor Fabri. '—that box—with his glove, missal, and seal.'

'You trusted the seal, such a valuable object, on such a journey?'

'Our priest, Father Cornelius, took the box to Eloise. He was accustomed to such errands. On his return, he assured us that he had delivered the box, then Eloise sent word that François's bequest had arrived.'

My aunt bowed her head and put her hand to her eyes. 'Take your time, Ghislaine.' Signor Fabri looked at her kindly. 'These are terrible memories, but I must ask you to go on. Did your brother François make a will?'

My aunt looked up at Signor Fabri and spoke clearly. 'He did, signor.'

'Did you see the will?'

'I did. Two copies were made. One was left here in the care of the prior. The other was handed to me to place in the box with the other items.'

'Do you know the terms of this will?'

'Yes. My brother François declared that his heir should be Eloise de Courcey, the mother of this young woman here. That Eloise should inherit La Paix.'

The hall shivered with gasps and excited whispers, so that Signor Fabri instantly warned that he would have the place cleared if the crowds could not be silent.

'That is a lie!' shouted Sir Gaston. 'She lies!'

My aunt clenched her fists and glared at him, and I became aware of a grumbling sound coming from the people at the back of the room. Hands closed tight on spade handles, fists clenched on hammers. My aunt had her own men-at-arms, her devoted retainers, who would set on any man who called her a liar, nobly born or not.

'That is a lie,' repeated Sir Gaston.

'Silence, Sir Gaston! You will have your say at the proper time.'

'So Eloise de Courcey was your brother's chosen heir?' My aunt nodded. 'For the court, out loud, if you please—'

'Yes.'

'And, in the event of Eloise de Courcey's death—'

'My niece, who stands before you, Mariane de Courcey—'

'She does not have the seal.' There was a cold smirk of triumph on Sir Gaston's face. I lunged at him. He shoved me back. As I stumbled, my aunt caught me.

'Order, order, Mariane de Courcey. This does not help your case.' Signor Fabri frowned at me, then slowly placed his hands either side of my father's things. 'Tomorrow the prior shall bear witness.'

CHAPTER TWENTY-NINE
JUSTICE

The hearing was suspended until the same hour the next morning. For the rest of that day I tried to put it out of my mind. Neither the sick in the infirmary, nor the herbs in the garden could wait for the outcome: mistress of La Paix or plain Mariane made no difference to them. But I was glad of tasks to keep my hands busy, and my head distracted from the blaze of my desire for revenge.

The night seemed endless as I tossed and turned in my bed. I held my knife close under my pillow and planned how I would use it, lying in wait for Sir Gaston behind the stable door at night when he came to look over his horses. I would borrow a monk's habit from the priory laundry, wearing black so as not to be seen. He would bluster into the stable and dismiss the grooms. We would be alone and as he raised his hand to stroke the mane of his favourite horse, I would plunge upwards—At this point my mind reared away from the finish as pictures of battle flashed before my eyes: I saw the dead, their bodies broken like the toys of a giant child, thrown down in ill-temper; I saw the man I had killed, curling up in his agony, his death moans filling my ears until I moaned myself.

Dawn woke me, so I must have slept, but I was

exhausted. I dressed and washed and walked into the hall, on feet of lead.

'We are all gathered?' Signor Fabri asked. My aunt nodded. 'We are all gathered, signor.'

We took up the same places as on the previous day, swore our oaths to tell only the whole truth, and waited for Signor Fabri to begin. Opposite me, Sir Gaston looked bored and impatient, tapping his finger on the back of the empty chair next to him.

Signor Fabri began to speak. 'I call Father Bernard, prior of La Paix. Father?' Signor Fabri paused as Father Prior emerged from the crowd at the back of the hall. He is my friend and I looked to him for a sign of greeting as he passed, but he kept his eyes on Signor Fabri, his hands tucked up and hidden in the long black sleeves of his habit. After he had taken his oath, Signor Fabri asked:

'Father Bernard, will you tell us what you know of the final hours of François de Louvier?'

'Of course, signor,' said the old man quietly. Silence fell in the hall, as we hung on to his words. Outside I could hear a robin call and the rush of the mill-race.

'François lay dying. He sent word to me to go to him and hear his confession. I was also to take writing materials to scribe his last wishes with regard to La Paix.'

'He wanted to dictate his last will and testament?'

'Yes, signor.'

'Did you scribe the will?'

'I did.'

'Tell us if you can, what was written in the document.'

The prior finally looked at me, but his eyes were dark

and unreadable. Then he looked at Gaston and said, 'François bequeathed La Paix to his lady, Eloise—'

'Lies!' shouted Gaston. 'You lie, prior! Show us the will. Show us the will.' Gaston looked round for support and his henchmen, who today had placed themselves among the crowd, echoed the call. 'The will! The will!'

'Gaston, my son,' Father Prior said with great patience. 'You know very well that you took it yourself from the priory.'

'But I have no will, prior.' With great mockery, Gaston spread his hands wide. 'Without it, everything depends on the seal, does it not? And so, with the seal—*my* seal—I stake my claim.'

The silence in the hall was like a held breath. Signor Fabri broke the tension. 'Ah yes. The seal,' he said. 'Now is the time for you to tell us, if you will, how it came into your possession.'

Sir Gaston sent an arrogant glance round the hall. 'There is no need for me to justify my claim. *She* comes to dispute it,' he said, pointing straight at me. '*She* says the seal is hers, that it was left for her by her mother who received it from François. This seal has travelled a merry journey!' He laughed and there were some who laughed with him, whether from loyalty or anxiety. 'The priest, Father Cornelius, whom you say took the seal to her, is unfortunately no longer with us, God rest his soul. So, by your word, François sent her the seal. By mine, he did not. If she still says she had it in her possession, then let her prove it.'

I burned with frustration. There was no proof. All the witnesses were dead. It was hopeless.

❦ 229 ❦

Signor Fabri waited, quite still, for silence, then he said, 'There were two witnesses to the fact that Eloise received the box from François. Come forward, Thérèse Laroche and Renée de Courcey.'

I spun round in shock to see my aunts, my mother's sisters, walking towards me from the back of the hall. I ran to them and tearfully embraced them. We kissed each other and hugged as if we would never be parted again.

'Mesdames, if you please,' called Signor Fabri. 'Attend the hearing.'

Reluctantly I let them go and went back to my place. They took their oath, then Signor Fabri began his questions.

'Thérèse Laroche and Renée de Courcey, you are sisters to Eloise, the mistress of François de Louvier and mother to the demoiselle Mariane who stands here for judgement?'

'We are,' they murmured.

'And neither of you has set eyes on your niece, Mariane, since she left Reims after her grandmother's death, nor has ever spoken to her about her inheritance?'

'No, signor,' my aunts replied, shaking their heads.

'Very well. Which of you will bear witness?'

'I will,' said my aunt Renée, stepping forward.

'Renée de Courcey, examine, please, this box and its contents. Have you seen them before?'

'Yes.'

'All of them?'

'Yes.'

'Including this?' Signor Fabri held up the seal.

'Of course. It is the de Louvier seal. When François sent

it to my sister, Eloise—' there were gasps in the room and my aunt stopped, puzzled.

'Go on,' said Signor Fabri.

'When Eloise saw the seal, she was terrified.'

'Why was that?'

'My sister knew at once what it meant and rejected such a grand inheritance. She loved François, but she could not live at La Paix.'

'Why did she not then return the seal to François's sister or to his brother, Gaston?'

Aunt Renée hesitated and glanced at Sir Gaston, before replying, 'François warned her to keep the estate out of his brother's hands at all costs. He knew what such power would do to him, how it would corrupt him and feed all his weaknesses. But Eloise feared to send the seal to Ghislaine, who would have to face Gaston alone, if ever he returned from England.'

'And the copy of the will that was sent? You saw it?'

'Yes. François sent it to Eloise. A copy of the original which he left here in the priory. The will came with the other things in the box. In it François specifically stated that La Paix should go to their child, after Eloise's death.'

'Where is the will now?'

'Eloise burned it. She thought it best.'

'All this was what? Fifteen years ago? What did Eloise do with the box all that time?'

'She buried it, signor. After François died, she tried to forget. She buried it.'

'Now, Renée, I want you to think carefully. Was the de Louvier seal in the box?'

'Yes, signor. It—'

Signor Fabri raised his hand. 'Pardon me, if you will, madame. I should now like to question Mariane.'

Signor Fabri raised his eyebrows to me and beckoned me forward. I stepped up to the bench. 'Will you show us, Mariane, how you discovered your father's seal?'

Aware that this could weigh the scales indisputably in my favour, I took up my father's glove and held it high, for all to see. My aunt stepped forward and from a leather bag at her waist, emptied out a mess of clay soil on to Signor Fabri's table. I scraped up some of the clay and rolled the seal up in it, then pushed the ball into the fore-finger of the glove. Then I shook the glove hard until the seal fell out again. I held the seal in the centre of my palm, rubbing off the clay to reveal the gold.

'Exactly, signor, that's what happened!' declared my aunt Renée. 'Eloise daubed the seal with clay and pushed it right into the tip of the glove, so that, at a cursory glance, no one would find it.'

'Lies! All lies! They are all in this together!' shouted Sir Gaston.

'Sir Gaston.' Signor Fabri's voice was like ice. 'I am the judge in this dispute. I alone. Speak only when you are spoken to.' With bad grace, Sir Gaston tossed his head and stood sullenly, with his arms clasped across his chest.

'Sir Gaston, I am unaccustomed to ask either side in a dispute of this kind for permission to hear certain evidence, but for your father's sake and the sake of your future dealings with Mariane de Courcey, I want you to see that here we are dealing only with what is lawful. Whatever takes place here is justice and my judgement is final, yes?' He waited for some acknowledgement and Sir Gaston, still sullen, finally nodded.

'Very well, do you agree to hear the testimony of one who knew nothing of the box, nothing of François de Louvier and nothing of the legacy. Do you, Sir Gaston, have any objection?'

Sir Gaston shrugged.

He took out a letter.

'I have here a letter of testimony from Jehanne d'Arc.' The words, echoed by many lips, ran round the hall like a whispering wind. Eyes wide, I stared at my aunt. 'It was Didier's idea,' she whispered. Signor Fabri began to read.

In her letter, Jehanne described how proud I had been of my father's seal and how I had worn it in battle beneath my glove as he had done.

As he lowered the letter I looked across at Didier, who grinned back at me.

'On the testimony before me, we must accept that François de Louvier did send the seal to Eloise de Courcey along with a copy of his last will and testament, and we must accept that Mariane here is her mother's heir. From the letter we see that the seal was in Mariane's possession. How it came to Sir Gaston remains a mystery, one which is not the concern of these proceedings.

'By law and justice, on the basis of the evidence here presented, I find for Mariane de Courcey and declare that her claim to inherit the estate of La Paix, the manor house—'

'But they were never married! The de Courcey woman was my brother's mistress, a Reims whore who spawned this bastard child—'

'Curb your tongue, my son.' The prior's voice cut through

Sir Gaston's speech. 'Your brother and Eloise de Courcey were married.'

I gasped and clutched my aunt's sleeve. Her hand closed over mine.

'I myself presided over their union in the holy sacrament of marriage, a union forced to be kept secret because your brother feared what revenge you would wreak in his absence. He knew you too well.'

'And I him. Milksop.' Sir Gaston's anger rose again. He thumped the table and shouted. 'I shall bring my own judge!'

Ignoring this outburst, Signor Fabri continued his summing-up in a clear measured voice.

'—the manor house, the land, farms and all that appertains thereto, stands firm, in accordance with the wishes of her father, François de Courcey. I declare Mariane de Courcey to be the sole true liege-mistress of the demesne of La Paix.'

At the door, amid the cheers that greeted this announcement, Sir Gaston stood, surly as a black demon. 'This is not finished,' he said. 'You!' he pointed at me. 'Watch for my return.' Then he looked at Didier. 'And you! Stay out of my way. If I set eyes on you again, your life will not be worth a candle.'

I withstood the hatred in his eyes and kept my head up as he walked out of the hall, swiftly followed by his men.

'I'll go after him,' said Didier, 'I'll make sure that he leaves.' But I shook my head, then ran myself to follow Sir Gaston and watch him and his men. I wanted mine to be the last face that he saw, if he looked back. He still owed me a debt, for my mother's death.

Hosts of people stood between us as he and his men mounted up in the yard. They were clapping me on the back, touching my hands and, truth told, hindering me as I tried to get near him. But finally I stood at the front of the crowd and went towards him alone.

I watched Sir Gaston rein in his horse while he waited for Laurent to lower the drawbridge. His men-at-arms were still scrambling to mount up and gather their gear, this sudden call to leave having taken them by surprise.

'Get on with it, you old laggard!' shouted Sir Gaston, striking Laurent with his right foot. I was watching him closely but I still cannot say for certain what happened next.

Sir Gaston spurred his horse to ride out, but the bridge was only half-lowered, so that there was a little gap, a small jump to make between bridge and dry land. Perhaps the horse stumbled. Perhaps it took fright at something. Did I imagine it, that Laurent gave the rope a great heave, shaking the bridge just as Sir Gaston came up for the leap? None of us can say for sure. All we know is that Sir Gaston was thrown headlong into the shallow moat, where he lay, face-down in the water. His neck was broken.

CHAPTER THIRTY
COMPIÈGNE

S ir Gaston's death knocked me breathless with anger:
fate had cheated me of my longed-for revenge. The
revenge dream was so fully-fledged in my mind, that
I could not believe it was over. Even when I stood at his
grave looking down at the freshly-turned earth, my back
pricked as if my enemy were standing behind me. I could
not endure it, I could not, and my best beloved friends,
my aunt Ghislaine and Didier, felt the brunt of my fury.

Nothing they did for me was right. They tiptoed round
me as if I were a fractious child. My demands were extreme:
I ate nothing but unblemished fruit and bread made with
the finest oil, then drank only the water from St Ann's
well, five miles away. For days I refused food altogether,
then ate a whole pie and a jar of honey, before venting
the lot into the moat. My hair was uncombed, my hands
and face dirty. Instead of rousing myself, I lay in bed until
after noon, then tore my dress and wore that, if I got
dressed at all. I went barefoot and my feet blistered. I
groaned and growled like a wild beast.

As August burned into September, my aunts Thérèse
and Renée, and the judge Signor Fabri, stayed on at the
priory, and I refused to acknowledge their presence, treating
any kindness with a look of blasting scorn.

Finally Didier came to say that my aunts and the judge

had to leave and would share the wagon. Signor Fabri would go back to Troyes and my aunts to Reims. In a petulant temper, I threw out my hands, palms upwards. *Why?*

'Because Signor Fabri's exhausted,' Didier said, in a steady voice, 'and your aunts are needed at 'ome, for the 'arvest.'

I dismissed him with a rude gesture and turned my back on him. But Didier swung me round to face him.

'You're a proper wild cat, ain't yer?'

I flung up my arm to slap him but he caught me and held me firm, making me listen, though I was struggling all the time to break free.

'I know what's wrong,' he said. 'You wanted to do it yourself, didn't you? Gaston's accident cheated you of your revenge.'

God forgive me, when he said that, I spat in his face. Didier still held on to me.

'Don't think I don't know how you set your heart on it. I've had the same feelings myself, many times.' I thrashed in his grip. 'Now you listen to me. Ain't no use screaming against fate. What 'appened, 'appened, and when you think about it with your rational 'ead on, you'll see that God did you a favour. You're no killer, Mariane. I've seen you in battle, remember. Stop fighting me and listen! You're not like Gaston. He could murder and torture, then go to the tavern and eat a 'earty meal. Is that what you want, to be like 'im?

'If your 'eart's set on it, yes, you could be. Yes, anyone can blacken their soul.' For the first time I stood still and listened. 'But it's 'arder for someone like you.' He relaxed his grip a little. 'It's against your proper nature. If you ever

❖ 238 ❖

took that path, you'd never recover. You're a 'ealer, Mariane: you mend fings, you don't destroy 'em.'

We looked at each other then he let me go. Slowly rubbing my wrist I sat down.

'Revenge is best left to God,' Didier went on. ''e knows what's best, an' 'e 'as 'is reasons. If you 'ad killed Gaston, you'd 'a' been full o' sin: pride and anger, for a start. That's not very nice, is it?' I looked up at Didier with surprise.

'You see, we down 'ere can only see in part: we can't never see the 'ole thing. Only God and 'is angels can see that. Having the better view, you see—' Didier solemnly pointed to the ceiling. '—from up there.'

At this, I gulped, then I laughed. And then I cried, sobbing as if my heart would break.

'Oh Gawd,' Didier said, kneeling in front of me and patting my hand.

I tried, I did, I tried really hard to do what was expected of me as liege-mistress of La Paix. My daily routine was now very different. I could no longer be a healer in the infirmary. As the figurehead of La Paix, I must be seen and everyone wanted to get a good look at me. Laurent and the brothers had established a meeting place in the manor, in an ante-room to the main hall. And there were so many meetings. Every day began with them; there were always voices demanding attention, always someone with a pressing problem. I was farmer, lawyer, shepherd to my flock, mother-confessor, sometimes just mother: it was no disadvantage that I had no voice, since other people did the talking. Sometimes, with Didier's help, I made a judgement, but most people went happily on their way, after simply being allowed to talk and have someone listen, spilling out their troubles, uninterrupted.

After the morning meetings I made the rounds of the villages and farms, attending to such matters as the winter food stores and the rebuilding of the manor, now that I was installed there. Everyone else was cheerful and busy, happy that the estate had a head again, and I tried to step into my father's shoes and be what they expected me to be. But all the time I wore a false face, a mask. La Paix was an island, cut off from the rest of the world. The war was a distant memory, mentioned now and then in the news of a passing pedlar, but for the most part ignored as the yearly routines continued unchanged. Life was easy. I had food, rest, warm clothing, good friends. But every night before I got into bed, I would open the lid of my box and look at my father's things and remember that he was a warrior, who fought for the safety of all France, not just this small corner, called La Paix. There were letters in the box too, letters from Jehanne. I read them over and over.

She first sent news in August that the king had granted Domrémy exemption from taxes. Jehanne was pleased about that. Then, in later letters, the news was more troubling.

As we proceed towards Paris, all towns fall to the king. So far, all is well. But Bedford worries me. He says that Charles is not the king of France and maintains his own title as Regent to the boy king Henry. There is no sign of him and it's a dangerous silence. I know he's waiting for us, watching as we approach the city, but the king refuses to give any orders for the attack. Ah, this game of catch-me-if-you-can is unnerving. Bedford will seize any chance to reverse all our success. He must be soundly defeated.'

In September came further news.

My friend, all attempts to defeat Bedford have failed, and we have lost Paris. This is a severe blow, but worse is that our efforts were doomed from the outset, and the king knew it. I believe now that he has been negotiating privately with the enemy for weeks, agreeing to leave Paris in their hands. My heart aches for it. There is further bad news. I have broken my sword—it was an accident—but men whisper of it as a bad omen. I shall have hard work to convince them that nothing has changed, that we are all in God's hands and must trust Him. But what if the king forsakes me?

When I read that cry for help I longed to go to her, but I was needed at La Paix, so I sent a hopeful reply, recalling Didier's words that sometimes we can only see in part. Perhaps God had His reasons for the king's treachery. Perhaps, in the end, it would be all for the best. I wrote cheerfully, but a shadow lay on my heart. Jehanne was tired and alone, and the king had his own ideas about the war now.

All through that long winter a secret fear gnawed at my mind. Did I know then that tragedy was on its way? Did I foresee it? Night after night I would wake and fret about Jehanne and, I think now, reading over her letters, that she herself sensed the slow movement of fate, like a trap closing. More and more she was left without orders from the king and had to sit kicking her heels for weeks on end, or take things into her own hands. There was something else that unsettled her too. More and more folk flocked to her, simply to touch her garments, or the heel of her shoe, or they blessed her shadow as she passed, calling her saint, and claiming that by some miracle she had healed them. Jehanne denied it all. She was deeply troubled by their actions, always careful to thank God for the healing, and refusing to take the credit. Every day her voices encouraged her and never faltered, saying that all was happening according to God's plan.

But as the new year grew into spring, I waited for her letters with my heart in my throat. At Easter she told me that her voices had given her a warning, that soon she would be captured and put to death. She could not escape it. It was her destiny. She must finally put down her sword and endure it.

Profoundly shocked I wrote back immediately saying I would leave everything and go to her, but her reply asked me to wait. She might send for me later, but at present she was still in the thick of daily battles and she was sure I was more use to France at La Paix.

Jehanne never wrote to me again. In May there came a letter from de Poulengy. Jehanne had been captured at Compiègne, pulled from her horse as she struggled in swampy ground. She was held prisoner at the chateau of Beaulieu near Noyon, a Burgundian stronghold.

I left at once, astride Lionheart, wearing my soldier's dress, with my simple pack on my back. Didier came to the gate and took my hand. 'Send for me if you need me,' he said.

CHAPTER THIRTY-ONE
CAUCHON

I was with Jehanne throughout her imprisonment, accompanying her from bastille to bastille, as the English commanders Bedford and Warwick, acting on behalf of their king, and Bishop Cauchon, who was their Burgundian puppet, brought the full weight of their power down upon her.

Cauchon. When I first caught sight of him in Rouen, my spirit quailed for Jehanne: I knew him from Reims. This man, this bishop, is a devil in disguise. When I saw him, looking in at the door of Jehanne's prison, I shook with fright and when he left I couldn't stop. All the horror I had felt when Father Cornelius left me to die shot through me, as if I had touched red-hot steel. Evil priests. You trust them as men of God, then they strike you down.

Afterwards, whenever he appeared, Bishop Cauchon didn't speak, but he looked at Jehanne with loathing and I guessed why. His was a personal hatred. He wanted to be the one to hear the voices. He wanted to be the saint: he, Cauchon, who, I'm certain, had never heard the voice of God in his life. How could he have? There was no sign of it: none of the joy Jehanne showed on her face whenever the voices had spoken to her, none of the anguish she felt when they were silent. Cauchon's spirit was too clogged with earthly things to hear the saints. He was too tied to the world. He lived, as grandmère said, with his nose stuffed in the trough of greed. He dressed in the finest cloth and rode the best horses. He ate costly food and drank the best wine. Poor Cauchon. He was just a man, like other men, but he pretended he wasn't and he was cruel and vicious too. Worse for us, in league with his masters, he had the power of life or death over Jehanne. So I knew from the beginning how it would end.

Rouen, in the heart of Normandy, English territory, was where they held her for long months of questioning. They called it a trial, accusing her of witchcraft, and assembled a fine array of the best judges, but it was all for show. The outcome was never in doubt. Warwick paid ten thousand livres for her and Cauchon took the blood money. Warwick, with the English king and nobility watching, strutted his hour on the stage. He gloried in her capture, the girl-soldier who had humiliated the English for so long. He was delighted to pay. At such a price, she would never be set free. The English would get rid of her, and all our dreams of a free France, by staging a public execution. They would kill Jehanne and show her body to her followers. With great ceremony they would tie her to a stake, raise her on high for all to see, then they would burn her.

The charge against her was heresy, on two counts: she claimed to foresee the future and she claimed to hear the voices of saints.

As if she were violent or dangerous, they kept her in a bare room, bringing in bedding every night and taking it away again every morning. They clamped her legs in irons and chained her by the waist to a great log. And there she sat for day after endless day, for weeks, for months, without complaint.

At first I was not allowed to stay with her, except for an hour or so every evening, when, at change of guards, one who was more friendly than the rest turned a blind eye. As the seasons passed, autumn, winter, Christmas, the regime relaxed. Was it from sympathy? Did the guards finally judge Jehanne for themselves?

She never faltered in her habits. She sat silent or talked to me, or prayed. She ate bread and drank water. She asked for nothing else. Often when her voices comforted her there was such radiance about her, as if she didn't see her cell or her chains at all, but in her mind, walked with them in paradise. All this was obvious to any onlooker. Her innocence was as evident as broad daylight. So, without comment, the guards let me stay.

I don't think Jehanne realized the final danger at first. One evening in January, when she had been a prisoner for eight months, we sat silently together, our hands clasped.

'God won't let me burn, will He, Mariane?' she said suddenly. 'He chose me and sent His saints to speak to me. He could set me free at any minute. He could break these chains.'

I froze, making no sign that I had heard her.

'Mariane?' she said.

When again I made no move, she let go of my hand and heaved her chains and rattled them. When I looked round, she was twisting her head over her right shoulder to watch the last ray of sunlight in the slit of blue sky, just visible in one of the windows.

The back of her neck was so dirty, smeared with mud and sweat. The rucked line of the scar of her wound was white by contrast. Her hair was ragged, thick with grime and grease. Irritably she reached up to scratch her scalp. Lice, no doubt.

'He won't let me be burnt,' she murmured, hugging her arms across her chest.

I reached out to comfort her, then let my hand drop as a soldier opened the door with a clang and jerked his head to say I must leave.

That night I didn't sleep and returned to the prison next day at dawn. Jehanne looked up as I walked into her cell. She had put on her red peasant dress, the symbol of her alloted place on this earth: farm girl, spinner, obedient daughter, obedient wife, ready to take up all the responsibilities and tasks decreed by custom. It was over. She had removed her men's dress. She had renounced her mission.

As I looked at her my heart broke to see her great spirit tamed like that of a blinded falcon. But I reached for her as she stood up to greet me, dragging her chains, and held her tight in my arms, hugging away all my grief and pity. She was my cousin Jehanne again from Domrémy. We who had shared so much would stay together now and grow old together, spinning thread and sharing the memory of these months as a fitful dream, or choosing to forget, as if they had never happened.

'They said if I took off my men's clothes and put on my gown, I should not be burnt. I have sat all night in my gown.' She gave a low laugh.

'What do you think God is like?' she said, pulling me down to sit with her on the floor. 'Some see Him as an old man in the sky, with a frown and a raised fist, like an angry father. But they mistake Him, Mariane.' She put her arm round my shoulders and rocked me. 'He's inside us, all of us, a guide, a map to guide us home. He's my inspiration, my breathing, my very blood. He's part of me. In here.' She tapped her chest. 'How can I deny Him? He moves in all things, all times, all places. In the earth, the air, the water. And, yes—in the fire. Oh, I am afraid. My body shakes to think of it. But my death, as my life, is His to command. God has called me to do this. I have no choice. I have to focus all my mind on Him and abandon my senses. Sometimes I can, when I'm strong enough. If I focus my entire mind and spirit on Him, I will be able to forget the body, which after all—poor body—is just a shell. Don't look so dismayed, Mariane. If you had heard God's saints speak to you as I have, you would be strong enough.'

She paused, then spoke again. 'Help me, Mariane,' she whispered, plucking at my sleeve. We broke apart as she began to undo the tags that laced her blouse.

With a growl I tried to stop her, but she held me back, then went on taking off her peasant's dress. 'I have no choice.' Her voice was a thread of sound, fragile as frayed cotton.

Then, standing before me in a plain white shift, she said, 'Here I stand. They must take me as I am. It is my destiny. I am God's messenger. Tell them, whoever asks, afterwards. Tell them, it is so.' Then she put on her soldier's dress again.

So, brave to the last, she submitted to them, to Cauchon and the English, and walked willingly to her death.

CHAPTER THIRTY-TWO
30 MAY 1431

The day of Jehanne's death dawned bright with sunshine in a cloudless blue sky, but I was numb to its beauty. As I made my way down to the *place* in the centre of Rouen, all the usual sounds of a busy summer morning in town rose up around me: the honking of geese, the whicker of horses, the yelp of dogs, the rumble of carts and the drone and murmur of market stallholders, setting out their wares. A horde of rogues and scoundrels arrived early, to stake out favourable positions, thinking to turn a good profit from the crowds of onlookers. I passed by like a ghost. None of it seemed real.

All the while hammer blows jarred my ears, from where joiners were erecting a scaffold to support the pyre. I struggled not to see it at every glance and, keeping my eyes fixed on the road out of the town, I went to stand in the doorway of the inn, where Didier had promised to meet me.

I had been refused permission to stay with Jehanne on her last night. Alone in my lodgings, I prayed and prayed, but nothing happened to save her. The hammer blows went on.

When cart after cart passed by, piled with bundles of dead wood, as if they had cut down a whole forest to burn her, my soul ached. *Where was Didier?* Then suddenly he was there, dabbing my forehead with lavender oil sent by my aunt Ghislaine and ordering strong ale to revive me.

De Poulengy and La Hire were with him. Moving apart from the gathering crowds, we sat side by side on a bench outside a pie shop and I took Didier's hand and pressed it. My face told him the rest.

'I'm sorry—yer know—about Jehanne. It don't seem right, not any way about, an' it's a terrible death, this—' I squeezed his hand once with a fierce grip, then let go and turned away. He took the hint. 'I wasn't meaning to upset you, Mariane.' I turned back to him, and seeing his anxious face, shook my head.

'Why don't you leave this place?' La Hire said. 'It isn't place to linger.' He took off his cap and wiped his hand over his forehead. 'There's nothing you can do. Come on, 'twould be best to leave.'

Didier nodded in agreement and took my arm, but, growling, I shook him off. 'Na . . . na . . . *na* . . . **NAGHHH**.'

De Poulengy seemed stunned by what was happening.

Folk turned to stare at Didier and me grappling and he let me go. 'All right, all right.' We sat down again.

'Will you come back to La Paix? When you're ready, that is?'

I offered him no answer, because just then I caught sight of the cart that was parting the crowds, bringing Jehanne to the square.

She stood at the back of it, dressed in a long black robe, her face tiny and white beneath a tight black scarf. A tall dour man stood beside her, also in black. Her executioner. I broke free of Didier and forced my way through until I stood right where the cart would pass. I had to let her know that I had not deserted her. I wanted her to know that I was there and that I would stay with her to the last. I had something to give her too, a draught of valerian, to dull the pain, if she would take it. As the cart approached I stood in its path and lunged for the horse's bridle.

'Hold hard, ho!' shouted the carter, as soldiers sprang to pull me away. One of them held me from behind in a tight grip, under my armpits, and was lifting me bodily away. At a nod from the man in black, he released me.

'Approach the cart,' the executioner said.

Onlookers had flocked there before me and were now trying to touch Jehanne. They plucked at her robe, kissed the hem and the cuffs of her sleeves. 'Clear away there,' said the executioner as I came close and, at the threat of raised swords, the crowd fell back. Jehanne, unmoving, still had not looked in my direction. *She'll pass by without seeing me*, I thought as the carter prepared to move on, but the executioner stopped him, dropping a heavy hand on his shoulder. As if she knew my fear, Jehanne turned and looked.

Our eyes met and she smiled, a calm slow smile, and held out her hand to me. I reached up and grasped it, then stood on the ledge behind the cartwheel and hauled myself up to her. She bent down to me, as far as her chains would let her move. 'Be brave,' she said, as if I were the one facing death. Quickly I pressed the valerian into her hand and gave her a brisk nod to say she must take it. She looked at the phial, then took a silver cross from around her neck and passed it to me in her closed fist. 'We'll meet in heaven,' she said, as the cart began to move again and I jumped down. 'I'll be waiting for you.'

As the cart stopped at the foot of the scaffold, I opened my hand to look at the silver cross. It was entwined round the phial. She had passed the valerian back to me.

I watched her climb the ladder to the scaffold, until she stood there alone at the top, steady and calm, as the executioner, when all the prayers were said, tied her to the stake. Someone pushed a cross up to her, one of the soldiers—bless his name—and held it so that she could fix her eyes on it. Didier put his arm round my shoulders. 'Do you want to leave now?' he whispered as the crowd in the square gradually fell silent. I shook my head. How could I leave? Jehanne could not. *Here I stand.*

As the fire took hold, racing up through the dry kindling, her words filled my head. *'If I focus my entire mind and spirit on Him, I will be able to forget the body, which after all—poor body—is just a shell . . . If you had heard God's holy saints speak to you, as I have, you would be strong enough.'*

In the end I am not sure that she was. She held up until the last thin, exquisite point of pain then, as the flames covered her face, I heard her cry out. It was a piercing explosion of sound that shook me to the root, that I will never forget, that haunts me still in my dreams.

Did she then stumble into heaven, with wild angry curses, shouting 'Why have you done this to me? Why?' Or was it in the long silence that followed the cry that she left? Did she escape then and rise up, like a wisp of smoke from her own funeral pyre, floating into heaven, already unfurling her angel's wings, iridescent in the glow of the flames?

Her death moved many of those watching. I saw a priest fall to his knees and beg God's forgiveness. A soldier shook his head and said, 'This is badly done. She was no witch.' A woman standing in front of me ran into the pyre and smeared her face with hot ashes. Some of the judges who condemned her bitterly regretted what they had done. You could see the shock on their faces.

Stunned and seared, I could not move from the site, in spite of all Didier's entreaties. I waited and watched until dark. The evil was not over with Jehanne's death. Some doused the fire and showed her remains to those who stayed to look. Then the fire was lit again, to burn her again. How did I stand it? Because I couldn't leave her— she, naked, scorched, dead, had no choice.

When the fire finally consumed her, the blasphemous dogs kicked her ashes into the Seine. But on the open wound of my grief, her words came to me again, falling like cool rain. 'The body is merely a shell. I shall be with God.'

As dusk fell and the crowds began to leave, I moved closer to the pyre, for one last look. Didier stood with me. Against the red sky, I saw a small dark speck blunder up from the ashes. I grabbed Didier's arm and pointed, my arm outstretched. I watched it rise through the smoke, at first a little clumsy, stumbling, black against the pink glow of the clouds, then it flew, sure and steady as an arrow, high into the darkness and its clear bright song burst over me.

'What is it, Mariane? What are you looking at?' said Didier. I tugged at him and pointed, willing him to see the lark, wanting him to hear it singing, but Didier didn't see it. In the end, when the lark was out of sight and hearing, I shrugged and dropped my arm.

CHAPTER THIRTY-THREE
LA PAIX, 1456

'**G**randmère?'

'Yes, *ma petite*?'

'I wish you didn't have to go.'

'Oh, but Paris isn't far. We'll be back in a month.'

'Why do you have to go?'

'To put right a great wrong.'

'Who is Auntie Isabeau?'

'She's Jehanne's mother, ma chère.'

'She's very old.'

'Yes, well, it all happened a very long time ago, which is all the more reason to put things right if we can. Maman and I will go with Auntie Isabeau to Paris, to the hearing, where people will find out the truth about Jehanne.'

'Will they burn Cauchon?'

'Bishop Cauchon, *trésor*. No, there will be no more burning. Bishop Cauchon was in grave error when he condemned Jehanne and he will suffer for it.'

'How?'

'That's up to God. But, look, the rooks are flying home to their nests in the treetops. It's bed time.'

'But—'

'Eloise, Eloise, into bed now, no more talk.'

I tucked the covers snugly round my granddaughter and bent to kiss her forehead.

'Grandmère?'

'Yes?'

'Will Granpa go with you?'

'Yes. He must bear witness to the miracle. Now, what about a story? Which would you like—"The Good Samaritan" or "The Lost Sheep"?'

'Tell me again about the miracle.' Her voice was already sleepy and her eyes half-closed.

'Again?'

'Yes.'

'Just once more then.' I settled myself in my chair and clasped my hands loosely in my lap. '*Eh bien*,' I began. "One night, when I was fast asleep, suddenly—"'

With her eyes closed, Eloise murmured, 'No. Tell it from the beginning, from "The days following the death . . ."'

'Ha,' I smiled and began again.

'The days following Jehanne's death were dreadful to me. Grandpa Didier and I rode back to La Paix in despair. You can't imagine despair, *ma petite*, but it's as if you have lost touch with God, you can't find Him anywhere, and everything loses its life and colour. Everything turns to ashes, like the ashes that were kicked into the Seine from Jehanne's funeral pyre. My food was without taste, my rest without comfort, my days grey and endless. And Didier suffered too, because I was lost to him. I retreated inside myself, as a snail stung by grit hides deep in its shell. Every night after our sad return to La Paix, I prayed for Jehanne's soul, but my prayers were just empty words.'

'You couldn't speak then.'

'No. I spoke my prayers in my mind.'

'Go on.'

'Well, one night, I finally fell into an exhausted sleep. I was so tired, so very tired. But then, after a while, I woke up, fresh and alert. There was someone in my room. A figure standing at the foot of my bed.'

'Who was it?'

'You know who it was.'

'I want you to say.'

'It was Jehanne. There she stood, glowing and gleaming in her silver armour, as she had looked at Orléans in the afternoon sun.'

'What did she say?'

'She called my name. "Mariane. Mariane."'

'Grandmère?'

'What is it, *ma petite*?'

'I like your name.'

'Thank you. And I like yours.'

'Eloise. It was great-grandmère's name, wasn't it?'

'Yes.'

'If anyone tried to kill me, grandmère, I would fight them off with my quarterstaff.'

'You would, *mignon*.'

'Go on with the story.'

'Where did I get to?'

'To where Jehanne called your name.'

'Ah, yes. "Mariane," she said and I shot up in bed. She smiled at me, with laughing eyes, and I felt her peace and her blessing on me. But her terrible death flashed again into my mind, like a taunting demon. Then Jehanne spoke again and this is what she said:

'"Tied, you have to surrender the body. But with your mind you can choose: either to die cringing with fear, or to seize the flames like the reins of a destrier and ride into the pain. You ride it, shouting, as if you fly into battle, then before long it's over, and you're rushing through to the other side, straight into the arms of God."

'She threw back her head in joy, and I was swept with relief, that, for Jehanne, death had not been, after all, a defeat. It had been a great victory.

'She lowered her head and looked at me, and came round the foot of the bed to get a little closer. When we were near, she reached forward and touched my lips, and as my mouth opened, I felt a stone leave my throat. It slipped into the palm of her hand. She held her hand out flat and we both looked at the stone, which gradually dissolved and disappeared. Then she turned and began to walk away, fading from sight as she went.

'I scrambled to the foot of the bed, clawing the air to keep her with me. And then I spoke. For the first time since my mother's death, I spoke again.'

'What did you say, grandmère?'

'I said her name. "*Jehanne.*"'

'So the stone was the stone of your grief when great-grandmère died and Jehanne took it away, so that you could speak again.'

'Yes.'

'I expect you were shocked.'

'Well, if grandmère wasn't shocked, I jolly well was—'

Eloise jumped out of bed and went to hug Didier who had poked his head round the door.

'I heard her calling my name and my hair stood on end! I fell out of bed and knocked the water jug all over me best night shirt! She's been nagging me ever since.'

'Go on with you,' I said.

'It's time,' he said to me and let Eloise go.

'Hurry home,' said Eloise. 'Here, grandmère, let me do that.' Eloise picked up my bag. I sighed—'You should be in bed'—but then I relented and let her carry the bag downstairs for me.

As Didier and I mounted the waiting horses, my daughter Françoise met us with a basket of food, which she strapped to my saddle.

'God speed,' she said. 'Come safely home. Give my love to Aunt Isabeau, Uncle Jacques, and Pierre.'

'Have rooms ready for them, won't you, *ma chère*? Look for us in a month. There's fresh lavender in the chest.'

'Don't fret, maman, we'll see to it. I pray that everything goes well in Paris.'

'It will,' I said.

'Has Jehanne told you so, grandmère?' said Eloise, putting her hand on my bridle.

I looked with love into my granddaughter's eyes. She is a healer like me, and a seer. She knows the Great Spirit of Good that is everywhere if you know how to see it. But, like me, she must learn to hide her knowings: in this age of ours, the Church is still quick to condemn what it does not understand.

'Jehanne would have loved you, child.'

'Pray for me, grandmère.'

'Always.' I gathered my reins.

AN HISTORICAL NOTE

March 1450   On the orders of Jehanne's dauphin, by then King Charles VII of France, the first enquiry is held into Jehanne's trial. Witnesses are called to the hearing.

May 1452   The Church reconsiders the evidence against Jehanne.

June 1455   The Pope grants permission to Isabeau Romee (Isabeau d'Arc), Jehanne's mother, to begin the process of rehabilitation for Jehanne. The rehabilitation was to clear Jehanne's name so that she could be declared innocent of all charges of witchcraft.

July 1456   Rehabilitation of Jehanne in the Archbishop's palace at Rouen. Her trial is declared full of errors. A handsome cross is to be placed on the site of Jehanne's death.

9 May 1920   Jehanne is canonized, becoming St Jehanne or, in English, St Joan of Arc.